Raymond Briggs
Blooming Books

Raymond Briggs
Blooming Books

Words by Nicolette Jones

JONATHAN CAPE • LONDON
in association with Puffin Books

RAYMOND BRIGGS
BLOOMING BOOKS

A Jonathan Cape Book: 0 224 06478 9

1 3 5 7 9 10 8 6 4 2

Design by Inge Willems

First published in the United Kingdom, 2003
by Jonathan Cape
an imprint of Random House Children's Books
61-63 Uxbridge Road W5 5SA

Random House UK Limited Reg. No 954009
www.**kidsatrandomhouse**.co.uk

A CIP catalogue record for this book
is available from the British Library

Printed in Germany

Contents

For my Mother and Father

Foreword

Within the first two weeks at Wimbledon Art School, I was dubbed a 'commercial artist'. As I was fifteen at the time, I had no idea what this meant other than it was intended to be insulting.

I knew nothing at all about Art or Fine Art painting and, at the time, had not even heard of Van Gogh. I had gone to art school to learn to draw so as to become a cartoonist. But I was soon told that cartooning was an even lower form of life than commercial art. Everyone was expected to be a Fine Art painter, so I was more or less pushed into painting. It took four years of Wimbledon, two years of National Service and two years at the Slade School to discover, slowly and painfully, that I was not a painter at all. I was no good with colour and disliked oil paint.

I liked drawing and was good at line and tone. I was also interested in the figure and, above all, what the figure was doing and thinking and feeling. For me, this is the main difference between painting and illustrating. The painter is primarily interested in colour and the shape he is making with the figures; the illustrator is interested in the storytelling aspect of the picture.

It took those eight years to discover I was barking up the wrong tree. If there had been more perceptive teachers around at the time, they might have seen I was a natural illustrator. They could have saved me a lot of wasted time and effort. I am still no good at colour and still dislike the sticky mess of oil paint.

Despite having done dozens of oil paintings and even sold a few, I have no wish to be part of that world. You reach so few people by that method compared with books.

But I feel I never quite fit in anywhere else either. At meetings of the Society of Authors or the Royal Society of Literature, I feel I am not a proper writer. I only write short texts for picture books; it's not real writing. Then, at meetings of the Cartoonists' Club, the tough Fleet Street and Wapping lot make me feel as if I'm Beatrix Potter.

The commercial nature of my work seems to have been there from an early age. At ten I wanted to be a 'reporter'. By thirteen this had changed to wanting to be a cartoonist. Both these jobs mean writing and drawing for printing and for a commercial purpose.

It seems odd that something so specific should have surfaced so early in life. Most children, I imagine, show a general interest in a subject; they are good at Art or English, but I had always wanted to write for the press or draw for reproduction.

Commercial corruption was inborn it seems. So here it is – a whole blooming bookful of Commercial Art.

RAYMOND BRIGGS
April 2003

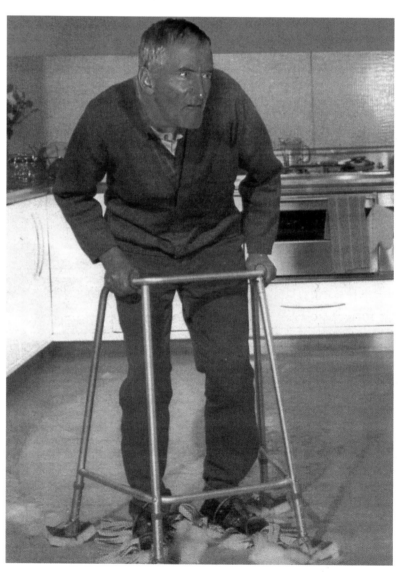

A recent portrait of Raymond Briggs by Alan Baker

Introduction

RAYMOND BRIGGS'S favourite judgement about himself was uttered by his partner Liz's granddaughter, Connie, at the age of three. She said: 'Raymond is not a normal person.' He wants this, he says, on his gravestone.

He is perhaps more normal than he cares to think. His greatest eccentricity is that he does not vaunt his success. He does not live as others might do if they had an international reputation, book sales in six figures, and rights sold in many different countries. He lives a quiet, industrious life, has occupied the same house in Sussex for thirty-six years (following the example of his parents, who inhabited theirs for forty-one), and drives an old car. Although he co-operates with the demands of publishers' publicity and marketing departments, he does not court celebrity. He turns down invitations to appear on radio or television when he doubts that he has anything significant to say. He does not enjoy having his photograph taken, but, though he grumbles about it and refuses to get into silly positions, he does not make life difficult for anyone with a camera and a job to do.

His life tends towards austerity. He travels rarely, a stranger to the merit of travelling hopefully, finding the discomfort and helplessness of getting there not worth the arrival. In this he is like his parents, who went abroad only once, to the Channel Islands, after they retired. (Father Christmas may be modelled on Briggs's father, but his holidays bear no relation to Ernest's experience.) Briggs broke with his own habit in 1998 and enjoyed himself much more than he expected when he went to Japan with half a dozen other illustrators whose work was included in an exhibition of English picture books. Briggs was bowled over by the hospitality and enthusiasm he encountered. 'They were queuing round the block for him at one appearance,' says his editor, Julia MacRae, who was among the party. 'Raymond looked at the crowd and said, "Who is this for?"'

Success has not tempted Briggs to accumulate fashionable trappings. He frequents charity shops for clothes, and likes to find bargains. One recent purchase (at the age of sixty-eight) is a pair of rollerblades in his size. 'Always fancied a pair, but they are so

Full-length oil portraits of his parents, Ethel and Ernest, in Raymond Briggs's living room

expensive. I couldn't resist these for £9.99.'

He has no computer, and communicates with friends and publishers mostly by faxing elegantly handwritten jocular letters. (All the staff in the publicity, marketing, editorial and design departments of his publishers have nicknames he has conferred upon them, and give as good as they get in exchanges of joshing faxes.) Friends used to say his pencil drawings were so much better than the inked-in finished illustrations. 'This was because inking in the first spontaneous pencil drawing often killed it stone dead. There are two ways of avoiding this: one is to continue the first drawing in pencil crayons so the colour gradually appears as the drawing goes on, or you can photocopy the pencil drawing into black and then work on that with water colour and crayon. Older photocopies used to put a sooty deposit on the paper which could be scraped off with a scalpel. Now, "improved" digital technology seems to embed the image into the paper, so scraping off is no longer possible. Life gets worse all the time, you see.'

His house, it is true, is not 'normal' in that it is not furnished and decorated in typical suburban style. The living-room ceiling is papered with a map of the British Isles. Full-length oil portraits of his parents adorn the doors of a cupboard in his living room. One upstairs wall bears an abstract composition made from the discarded blue plastic ovoids that packaged the ends of pipes laid by the Water Board outside his house. A promotional plastic relief of Fungus overlooks the lavatory, complete with speech bubble saying 'Fungus smells you'. Briggs exchanges lavatorial jokes with his friends – three of them have sent him copies of the German bestseller *The Mole Who Knew It Was None of His Business*, about a mole who wakes with a turd on his head and searches other animals' faeces for a match. In his studio, Briggs has a life-size papier-mâché model, made by friend Alan Baker for his fiftieth birthday, of himself on the lavatory. (His birthday, incidentally, is an auspicious day for children's books: he shares it – January 18th – with A. A. Milne and Arthur Ransome.)

He also has a weakness for unconventional collections, though he is trying, he says, to give them up. 'Collecting is almost a minor mental illness,' he says. He has collected, in his time: jigsaws of the Queen Mother, electric fires, plastic filter coffee lids, Mrs Mills LP covers, books with titles like *When the Wind Blows*, copies of *Just William* and *Robinson Crusoe*, posters with bathetic headlines from the local paper ('Five Pairs of Shoes to Be Won', 'Tea Party for Old Folks – Picture', 'Lewes OAP Found Dead') and 'oompah-oompah music sung by Germans in lederhosen'. Peculiar as some of these collections have sounded when reported in print, they originate in logic or jokes. The coffee lids were a literary reference – 'measured out my life in coffee spoons' – from T. S. Eliot's 'The Love Song of J. Alfred Prufrock'. Now that they reach from the side of his bath to the ceiling, making a striped tube Carl André might have been proud of, he has stopped collecting. The electric fires were a question of finding one he needed, and then seeing others of a more pleasing design. The jigsaws of the Queen Mother began with a jokey gift for Alan Baker who couldn't possibly want it. But he put it together, and then 'it seemed a pity to waste all that work'. He found four others, and now all five are framed on a wall. The fun of collecting the *When the Wind Blows* books (such as Walter de la Mare's *The Wind Blows Over*) was the pleasure of chance discoveries, until it was spoilt for him by a misguidedly helpful bookshop assistant who printed out a list of every related title from the internet. 'Now I know what they all are, there's no point.'

Briggs cultivates a curmudgeonly manner – 'I have a reputation for being grumpy, so I do my best to keep it up, but it's hard work,' he says – but his style permits expression of his deadpan humour. Occasionally, it has misled interviewers into calling him morose. He will make misanthropic pronouncements (that he dislikes Christmas, for instance) which have their roots in a dislike of ostentation, commercialism and affectation, but as a friend and host he is kind and polite. Those who know him well call him a sweetheart behind his back.

During his years of teaching at Brighton College of Art he was, his students report, enormously encouraging. Chris Riddell, the political cartoonist and award-winning children's book illustrator, is a former student. Briggs was his personal tutor from 1982 to 1984. 'We would look forward to his tutorials. He was so positive, he would make us feel fantastic. You came out walking on air.' He was also, says Riddell, a wonderful teacher by example. Riddell remembers that when

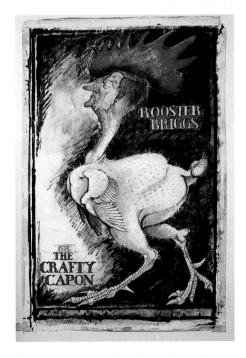

Birthday greeting from Sean Hetterley

Drawing by Sydney Moon of the *Sunday Dispatch*, 1947

Illustration by A. B. Payne, creator of *Pip, Squeak and Wilfred*, drawn for Raymond Briggs in 1947

The Tin-Pot Foreign General and the Old Iron Woman was published, 'I was very influenced by it in terms of thinking what one could do. It was possible both to be a satirist and to illustrate children's books. It was not a huge leap because Raymond had shown that the two worlds were merged.'

Briggs, who 'went to bat for students he believed in', championed some students, Riddell included, whose work he admired and who happened to be cartoonists. He would not allow their work to be treated as a lesser genre when it came to grading degrees. He believes the art of the strip illustration is particularly undervalued in Britain. 'I like to think that those of us he supported went on to vindicate his judgement,' says Riddell, 'and we are passing on what he taught us.'

Children's books were never, however, what he set out to work in – 'It was just a way of making a living' – and it is ironic that as a child he 'hated being given books'. At thirteen he started to draw, and was influenced by *Punch* magazine and newspaper cartoonists. He would write and ask for samples of work – something children would not get away with now. Several cartoonists obliged. He still has drawings by 'Moon' of the *Sunday Dispatch* and A. B. Payne, who drew *Pip, Squeak and Wilfred*. Arthur Ferrier, Lee from the *Evening News*, and 'Fougasse', aka Kenneth Bird, art editor of *Punch*, also responded generously.

Now he draws in the upstairs studio that he built onto his house, with its distant views over fields. 'I once kept a record of the time it took to do two pages,' he says. 'Pencilling – twenty hours, inking – eighteen hours [if he does this], colouring – twenty-five hours. And all that's after months of getting ideas, writing and planning.' Finished pages of picture books line a wall of his studio, while he thinks about changes.

Although Briggs's style is to make such pronouncements as 'middle age is awful, and it gets worse', he has reasons to be cheerful. He has a partner of thirty years. She has her own house, and they live semi-separately, but Briggs is an honorary grandparent, and close to her children and grandchildren, who have been an influence on his work. This is especially evident in his latest book, *The Puddleman*, which was inspired by a remark made by four-year-old Miles, looking at a depression in the ground: 'They haven't put any puddle in that one.' Briggs invented a man who puts in the puddles. As in *The Bear*, only the child hero knows the magical character exists. Adults – in this case Briggs himself, as the grandfather (in a characteristically unflattering self-portrait) – doubt it.

Briggs has reached an age when time passes too quickly. In his contribution to John Burningham's anthology, *The Time of Your Life*, he wrote, 'I had a party for my fiftieth birthday and another for my sixtieth, three or four years later.' But his creativity is unflagging. He keeps promising himself, he says, to give up the work, but already, as the pages of *The Puddleman* are being sent to his publisher, he has embarked on another picture book.

Fungus the Bogeyman's face is familiar to people who were not born when he first appeared in print. *The Snowman* is recognized in countries where it never snows. *When the Wind Blows* affected the way a generation thought about nuclear weapons. The use of strip cartoons in children's books is common now in a way that it was not before *Father Christmas* was published. Such is the impact of Raymond Briggs. His work has elevated the standing of the art of strip illustration and added status to children's books.

Briggs is modest about his work, although he sets himself (and production departments) the highest standards. He was once despatched, along with a group of other students, to the National Gallery, to compare some of his work to the paintings of masters. It was meant to be an inspiring experience. Briggs held one of his pictures up against Chardin's *The Lesson*, and got depressed. 'Next to the glowing luminosity and glory of Chardin, my picture looked and felt small, mean, and dirty; almost disgusting. I felt embarrassed and ashamed.' The critic Philip Hensher described Briggs's work as 'instantly recognisable, both in its warm look, and in its serious moral world. It is peculiarly English – his attractively fuzzy style draws . . . on a line of beautifully domestic and idealistic English artists, going back through the great Edward Ardizzone to Samuel Palmer.' Which is better than being normal.

From *The Puddleman*

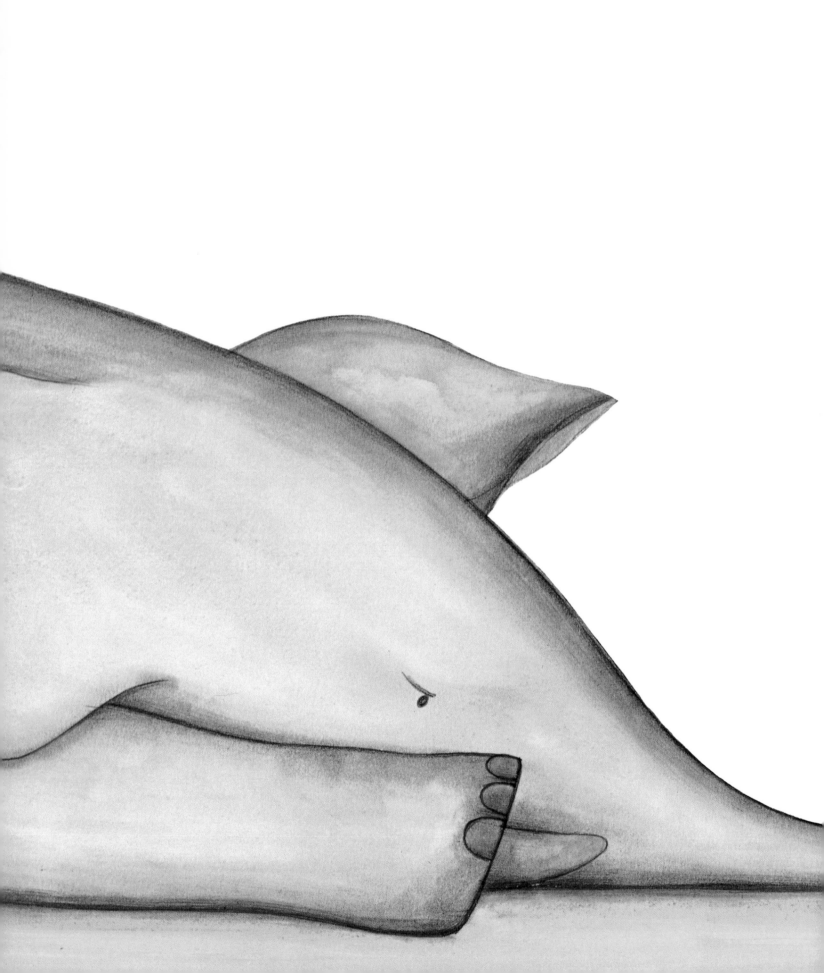

The Early Years

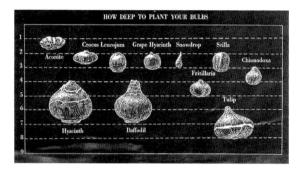

First piece of commissioned artwork for
House and Garden magazine, six guineas.
Scraperboard, 1957

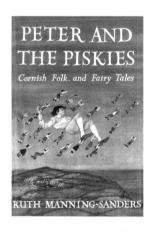

From *Peter and the Piskies*

EVEN AT ART SCHOOL, where it was not a highly valued skill, Raymond Briggs had a talent for drawing from memory, a prerequisite for being an illustrator. The essence of this talent, he says, 'is to be a mini-actor. If the figure is to crouch low in fear you have to feel that from the inside, like an actor. At the same time you have to be observing the figure from the outside and how it looks from your chosen point of view. Psychologically you have to be in two places at once. It's an odd business really.'

Raymond Briggs's first published illustration was for a magazine article. It was called 'How deep to plant your bulbs'. He drew a labelled cross-section of bulbs and earth, and an indoor scene of potted plants. He laughs at the mundanity of this, but in fact the skill of his draughtsmanship is apparent even in this simple subject.

After he left art school in 1957, Briggs tried to get illustration work from advertisers and magazine, newspaper and book publishers. One day he went to the Oxford University Press with some samples of work and was asked by editor Mabel George, who liked his work: 'How do you feel about fairies?' He managed, he says, 'not to swear', though he was thinking, You've done two years at the Slade and four years at Wimbledon and you're supposed to be a painter. Has it come to this? What he said aloud, swallowing his pride, was: 'Yes, fairies, lovely,' and in fact he went on to discover that fairy tales were 'the finest things to illustrate – there's nothing better really. Full of giants and fairies and animals talking. And they're usually set in the past so you don't have to draw boring modern things like cars. It's thatched cottages and costumes you can make up.' It became a favourite genre, together with nursery rhymes.

The first book Briggs illustrated, *Peter and the Piskies: Cornish Folk and Fairy Tales* by Ruth Manning-Sanders, was published in 1958 with black-and-white pictures of giants, mermaids, witches and devils. Briggs never met the author, who had been a poet and a novelist for nearly forty years and in the 1920s had travelled with a circus. The association with Briggs was fortunate for both of them. *Peter and the Piskies*, with its retellings of legends local to Penzance, where Ruth Manning-Sanders lived, was her first bestseller. Briggs went on to illustrate two more books she edited: *The Hamish*

Hamilton Book of Magical Beasts (1965) and *Festivals* (1972). On her 100th birthday, in 1988, he wrote and sent a copy of *The Snowman*. Her thank-you letter said, 'It does seem strange that we have never met, yet I feel that I know you from your pictures.'

The same year, he went to Hamish Hamilton to show his work, and editor Richard Hough responded favourably. Thus began an association with the publisher that has lasted, through the company's takeover by Penguin, for forty-five years. Beginning with Barbara Ker Wilson's *The Wonderful Cornet* (1958), Briggs illustrated eight other novels in the Hamish Hamilton series of books for 8–11s called Antelope Books. The best known among these authors were William Mayne (*Whistling Rufus,* 1964) and Alan Ross. *Whistling Rufus* is notable for the exceptional tenderness of Briggs's drawings of children.

Some of Briggs's illustrations for Antelope Books, contemporary though they were in the sixties, now look dated: the hero of *Peter's Busy Day* by A. Stephen Tring, for instance, wears a tank top, a short-sleeved shirt with a tie, rather snug shorts and long socks. But the books gave him an opportunity to draw some memorable images, whose appeal has in many cases outlived that of the texts, though even these have their enduring moments. James Aldridge's *The Flying 19*, published in 1966, begins, as it could if it were written now: 'It was a cold day in November and everything was normal in London. The traffic was jammed everywhere, from Battersea to Bermondsey. Everybody was late for work and school, everybody was angry and upset.' This book is enhanced by a wealth of characterful Briggs faces in the street and in bus queues, and *William's Wild Day Out* by Meriol Trevor (1963) is graced with energetic and delightful drawings of its springer spaniel hero, reminiscent of Peggy Fortnum's scrawly and charming pictures of Paddington Bear.

Not all of Briggs's illustrations were enthusiastically received by the authors. (Nor did he always admire their writing; some of it, he says, was 'terrible'.) Mabel Esther Allan, author of *The Way over Windle* (1966), later complained, inexplicably, that her characters, as portrayed by Briggs, looked like 'hideous, ninety-year-old dwarfs'. Looking at the pictures now it is hard to see what could have made

1. & 2. *Whistling Rufus*
3. *The Flying 19*
4. *The Way over Windle*

I
Tadpoles and Golf Balls

GERRY MARTIN and his friend Tim Rogers were out to look for tadpoles. Despite the sunshine Tim was feeling unhappy about going.

"I don't like the idea," he said. "It's not worth getting caught."

"Oh it's all right, Tim, we're not going to do any harm," replied Gerry. "We're only going just inside the wall where it's all overgrown. They won't mind that because they play golf much farther in."

7

He turned and slid wildly down the roof. A slate came loose and went clattering down.

"Ah!" came a triumphant shout from the doorway as the door burst open.

Gerry almost dived over the parapet, flinging himself straight at the trunk of the tree, not bothering with the branch. He twined himself about the trunk and slid down. Dust flew in his face and the bark grazed his check and knees. Suddenly he stuck.

He looked down and found that a spiky broken branch had gone right through his trousers, scratching his leg. He feverishly pulled the cloth free of the spike. As he regained his hold on the tree, he looked towards the house, and there, staring at him through the grimy window pane, was a pale, ghostly face.

47

1. *The Way over Windle*
2. & 3. *The Strange House*

18

her say so. Perhaps Briggs, unlike Ms Allan, was ahead of his time. At any rate, the book received the best reviews she had ever had.

Two years into the experience of illustrating other people's texts, Briggs thought he might have a go himself. 'I had a bash at one and showed it to an editor to get some advice, and to my amazement they said they would publish it. It staggered me. I knew nothing about children or children's books. It showed,' he says, self-deprecatingly, 'what the standard was.' Briggs had two books published in 1962 that he wrote and illustrated himself: *Midnight Adventure* and *The Strange House*. Both were stories of boys' adventures based somewhat on his own experience of going exploring at the age of about eleven to thirteen. 'In those days, post-war, we explored bombed houses, which were the most wonderful playground. You could do as much damage as you liked. Though of course we shouldn't have gone into them at all. They were terribly dangerous. The stairs could collapse, or slates fall off the roof.' *Midnight Adventure* involves boys who go fishing at night and come across burglars at a local golf club. Briggs never went out at night, but, as *Ethel and Ernest* later revealed, he was himself the burglar at his local golf club: as a boy he was caught breaking and entering and was brought home by the police.

The Strange House is based on a huge, abandoned house that was close to his home in Wimbledon Park. 'In my childhood it belonged to a Russian count, and stood empty except that an old Russian lady used to check on it, and she would chase us away shouting (in a thick Russian accent), "Criminal brains!" We broke into a semi-basement room, and there was a marvellous collection of birds' eggs in cabinets all around the walls. There was also a tunnel that came out on the golf course. And in the garden under the cypresses there were two ancient abandoned cars, an Edwardian Rolls-Royce and a Daimler-Benz.' Briggs as a boy sat in them and pretended to drive. Just as, later, the Snowman and the boy were to play in a stationary car.

Briggs designed the jackets for these two books, with decorative line drawing framing the title. On *Midnight Adventure* the decoration featured a vignette of two boys in raincoats and wellingtons by a pond. Briggs points out 'an interesting bit of sociology': that in a later edition, with a jacket by another hand, the boys wore pullovers and wellingtons. Later still they were in T-shirts and jeans. 'By then that's what boys their age had to be wearing. Raincoats would have been very uncool. But they were out in the middle of the night. They'd have frozen to death.' The photo-realist full colour that replaced Briggs's jackets was not only less well prepared for the weather but also uglier than the originals and deprived them of the period flavour that was part of their charm. As in many of Briggs's later picture books, his images evoked the time of his own childhood. Briggs wrote and illustrated another Antelope Book of his own, *Sledges to the Rescue*, in 1963, about helping a milkman on his round in the snow.

During the first ten years of his career as an illustrator, Briggs also drew skilled and detailed pictures of architecture for several books of non-fiction: Alfred Duggan's *Look at Castles* and *Look at Churches* (1960 and 1961) and Clifford Warburton's *The Study Book of Houses* (1963). Despite his talent for drawing from memory, he also did his time as a scrupulous producer of observational drawings.

At this point in his career, Briggs embarked upon four full-colour nursery rhyme books (*The Mother Goose Treasury* winning the Kate

almost dry and began smearing it on his face. 'Here, Tim, have some.'

Tim put down the bags and dipped his fingers in the mud. 'You don't need much,' said Gerry as Tim began plastering it on. 'Just one or two smears to break up the shape of your face.'

'Look out!' cried Tim suddenly. He pushed Gerry backwards into the grass as a train rattled along the top of the embankment. Its windows shone patches of light down the slope, and Tim and Gerry lay still as the light flashed over them.

26

'We're in full view of those houses,' whispered Tim.

'Oh, they'll all be asleep by now,' replied Gerry, as the train faded into the distance. 'Let's get into the stream.'

27

'Can't hear anything,' whispered Tim.

'No, I think it's all right.' Gerry ran on tip-toe across the path and vanished into the shadow of the hedge. Tim followed silently, and together they crept past the tea pavilion, jumped the low, wooden fence, and ran up the slope to the lake.

'What about going just the other side of those railings?' said Gerry, as they saw them through the trees.

'That's the golf course woods,' Tim replied.

32

'Yes, but it's where they all fish,' said Gerry. 'It's deeper there.'

'All right,' said Tim. 'Give me your rod, I'll put them through.'

'There are horrible great spikes on the end,' Gerry whispered. 'Mind your wellingtons.'

Tim followed Gerry out over the lake, holding on to the curving spikes and standing on the very edge of the rail with just the tips of his toes. The row of iron spikes was only an inch or two from his face as

33

From *Midnight Adventure*

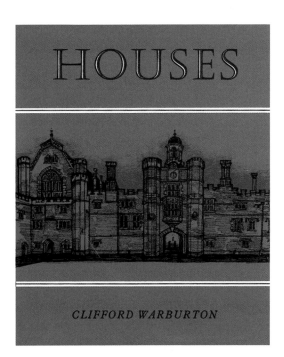

From *The Study Book of Houses*

When a terrible disease called the Black Death appeared in 1348, nearly half the people in England died. Many manors had no men left to plough and to sow. But the wool from English sheep was in great demand by merchants all over Europe. So instead of tilling their fields, farmers began rearing sheep.

The farmers grew rich and built new houses. They built them on the pattern of the manor house.

TUDOR, STUART & GEORGIAN HOUSES

☆ Small towns grew larger, and new towns sprang up. Craftsmen made all kinds of goods and more and more trading went on. So more houses were needed for the new dwellers in towns.

The houses were built close together in narrow streets. They were built taller and with upper storeys. Some were very beautiful. But behind the streets there were many poor, mean dwellings.

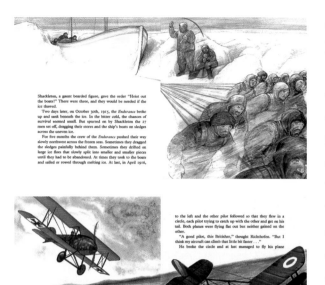

Shackleton, a gaunt bearded figure, gave the order "Hoist out the boats!" There were three, and they would be needed if the ice thawed.

Two days later, on October 30th, 1915, the *Endurance* broke up and sank beneath the ice. In the bitter cold, the chances of survival seemed small. But spurred on by Shackleton the 27 men set off, dragging their stores and the ship's boats on sledges across the uneven ice.

For five months the crew of the *Endurance* pushed their way slowly northwest across the frozen seas. Sometimes they dragged the sledges painfully behind them. Sometimes they drifted on large ice floes that slowly split into smaller and smaller pieces until they had to be abandoned. At times they took to the boats and sailed or rowed through melting ice. At last, in April 1916,

two machine-guns that fired forward through the airscrew. At the age of 23, Richthofen had already won ten aerial battles. Now he searched for an eleventh victory.

He looked again. Above him were three British aircraft! One of the pilots was coming for him, throwing his D.H.2 fighter into a fast gliding dive. "He will try to get behind me," thought Richthofen. "Let him try . . ."

The British aircraft opened fire. Richthofen swung his plane to the left and the other pilot followed so that they flew in a circle, each pilot trying to catch up with the other and get on his tail. Both planes were flying flat out but neither gained on the other.

"A good pilot, this Britisher," thought Richthofen. "But I think my aircraft can climb that little bit faster . . ."

He broke the circle and at last managed to fly his plane

Top: from *Shackleton's Epic Voyage*
Above: from *Richthofen the Red Baron*

Greenaway Medal) but these will be considered in detail in the Nursery Classics section.

After *The Mother Goose Treasury* won the Kate Greenaway, Briggs's editor Richard Hough had the idea that the spotlight the prize threw on Briggs's work would help to draw attention to a series of non-fiction books he had long hoped to publish. Six 'Briggs Books' came out, aimed at boys, and retelling the stories of real adventurers. Hough, who was an enthusiast for racing cars, wrote two of the books himself under the pen name of Bruce Carter. Their heroes were the racing drivers Nuvolari and Jimmy Murphy. Briggs found himself after all drawing 'boring modern things like cars' – which he did with an energy and sense of speed that owes something to the Italian Futurists. This is despite the fact that the cars he was drawing then achieved, as the text enthuses, 'top speeds of 53 mph'. Briggs got his chance at planes and ships too, with books on Lindbergh and Shackleton, as well as the story of Hillary's ascent of Everest, and (Briggs's least favourite) of Richthofen, the Red Baron. Briggs describes the man as 'a killing machine'. He dutifully drew the room Richthofen had lined with the numbers cut from the planes he shot down, and its chandelier made from their engines, but he points out in disgust that each of these numbers and engines 'represented a death'. This was not comfortable territory for the artist who went on to take an anti-war stand in *When the Wind Blows* and *The Tin-Pot Foreign General and the Old Iron Woman*. The Briggs Books are conscientious pieces of work, often introducing moments of humanity (as in the faces of Shackleton's men) into the *Boy's Own* spirit. But the freedom and imaginative possibilities of *The Mother Goose Treasury* were much closer to the course his work went on to follow.

FIRST UP EVEREST

RAYMOND BRIGGS Text by Showell Styles

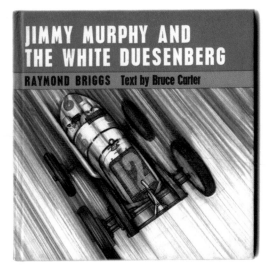

JIMMY MURPHY AND THE WHITE DUESENBERG

RAYMOND BRIGGS Text by Bruce Carter

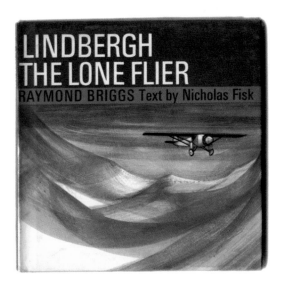

LINDBERGH THE LONE FLIER

RAYMOND BRIGGS Text by Nicholas Fisk

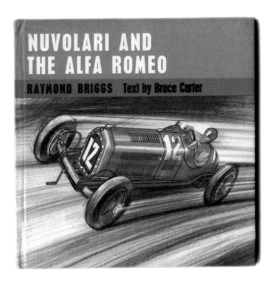

NUVOLARI AND THE ALFA ROMEO

RAYMOND BRIGGS Text by Bruce Carter

RICHTHOFEN THE RED BARON

RAYMOND BRIGGS Text by Nicholas Fisk

SHACKLETON'S EPIC VOYAGE

RAYMOND BRIGGS Text by Michael Brown

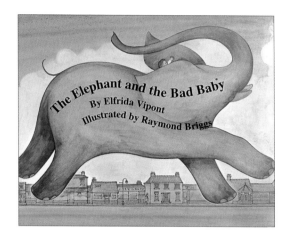

The Elephant and the Bad Baby (1969)

Briggs has illustrated only a few full-colour picture books that were written by someone else. One happy collaboration, whose popularity has endured since 1969 and taught generations to say 'rumpeta, rumpeta, rumpeta', was *The Elephant and the Bad Baby*, by Elfrida Vipont, another of whose books, *Stevie* (1965), Briggs had also illustrated. It tells the dream-like and episodic story of a baby riding on the back of an elephant who steals treats and is pursued by angry shopkeepers until they all go home happily to tea. In the middle, the kleptomaniac elephant accuses the baby of never saying 'please'.

'I never quite understood that,' says Briggs. 'The baby is supposed to be bad because it doesn't say please, but the elephant is a thief, always stealing things.' He thinks that a more apposite title would be *The Bad Elephant and the Baby*: the baby behaves as babies do – it wants the nice things it is offered, and couldn't really be expected to resist. A certain moral anarchy in the text makes Vipont an interesting counterpart to Briggs, in whose own books, where there is conflict between protagonists, it is never clear-cut who is wrong and who is right. One critic, Joanna Carey, found that 'the baby, a demanding little bruiser, with a mop of red hair, bears an interesting resemblance to Briggs's subsequent 1992 creation, the Man'. Like the baby, the Man is driven by his needs and appetites. The Man is, similarly, not necessarily bad.

Briggs illustrates this book from two points of view: with the eyeline low down on the page as if from a baby's height, to emphasize the size of the elephant, and with the eyeline higher than normal, as if the reader is up on the back of an elephant too. From this elevated height the reader can see more than the characters who are depicted: especially the visual jokes – the ladies' hats which resemble, from above, the pork pies or cream cakes their wearers are purchasing. Meanwhile the elephant's thefts go unobserved by all the preoccupied adults in the pictures, but children in the butcher's shop, the fish-and-chip shop, the grocer's and the sweet shop watch his crimes delightedly. Children inside and (as readers) outside the book are the privileged viewers, with the advantage over the adults. This is not implicit in the text: it is part of Briggs's contribution, and doubtless one of the reasons why this book engages small children so successfully.

Briggs also makes good use of the stop-start motion of the story: a theft followed by a chase. On the left, colour pages show the elephant loitering with intent at each shop. Below the text on the right, black-and-white drawings depict the pursuit. The drawings have a wild sense of motion, and in each case the elephant is incomplete, disappearing off the page. As the trail of pursuers gets longer, we see less and less of the elephant, creating a sense of movement, like a flick book, and conveying the impression that he is getting harder to catch. It also drives the reader to turn the page over. It makes this a picture book about the progression of a story: the chase and the development of the narrative are going in the same direction.

One picture was affected by the requirements of an American co-edition. Briggs drew a fish-and-chip shop, which would not have been familiar to American readers. Briggs saw no reason why this mattered – 'It would have been educational for them'– but bowed nevertheless to the pressure to make an alteration: 'I didn't want to draw it all again, so I drew the shop changing hands.' A painter up a ladder is painting out the 'Fried Fish' sign, and a notice says, 'Under New Management'. Another announces that the premises 'will open as Sam's Super Snacks'. The new business, which sounds American and modern, does not entirely suit the rest of Briggs's scene-setting.

Mostly the book is drawn as if the story is set in the 1940s, with the ladies in hats and tailored coats, the grocer with a collar stud attaching his collar to his shirt, and the butcher in a straw hat and striped apron. Briggs drew a fantastical Edwardian ice-cream stall with a moustachioed Italian serving cornets, giving himself licence for blithe anachronism and the use of any visual types he pleased. Hence the barrow boy on the fruit stall, who is, as Briggs admits, 'a modern spiv', dressed in the jeans, purple patterned shirt, wide tie, broad-lapelled double-breasted jacket and two-toned saddle shoes of the late sixties, when the picture was produced. With him the 1940s period detail has evaporated. But after all, readers of under five never have a very precise grasp of the history of costume.

The Elephant and the Bad Baby

Story by ELFRIDA VIPONT
Illustrations by RAYMOND BRIGGS

Hamish Hamilton · London

1

3

Once upon a time there was an Elephant.

And one day the Elephant went for a walk and he met a Bad Baby.
And the Elephant said to the Bad Baby, "Would you like a ride?"
And the Bad Baby said, "Yes."

So the Elephant stretched out his trunk, and picked up the Bad Baby and put him on his back, and they went rumpeta, rumpeta, rumpeta, all down the road.

Very soon they met an ice-cream man.
And the Elephant said to the Bad Baby, "Would you like an ice-cream?"
And the Bad Baby said, "Yes."

  So the Elephant stretched out his trunk and took an ice-cream for himself and an ice-cream for the Bad Baby, and they went rumpeta, rumpeta, rumpeta, all down the road, with the ice-cream man running after.

9

11

Next they came to a pork butcher's shop.
And the Elephant said to the Bad Baby, "Would you like a pie?"
And the Bad Baby said, "Yes."

   So the Elephant stretched out his trunk and took a pie for himself
and a pie for the Bad Baby, and they went rumpeta, rumpeta,
rumpeta, all down the road, with the ice-cream man and the pork
butcher both running after.

Next they came to a baker's shop.
And the Elephant said to the Bad Baby, "Would you like a bun?"
And the Bad Baby said, "Yes."

   So the Elephant stretched out his trunk and took a bun for himself
and a bun for the Bad Baby, and they went rumpeta, rumpeta,
rumpeta, all down the road, with the ice-cream man, and the pork
butcher, and the baker all running after.

13

15

Next they came to a snack bar.
And the Elephant said to the Bad Baby, "Would you like some crisps?"
And the Bad Baby said, "Yes."
   So the Elephant stretched out his trunk and took some crisps for
himself and some crisps for the Bad Baby, and they went rumpeta,
rumpeta, rumpeta, all down the road, with the ice-cream man, and
the pork butcher, and the baker, and the snack bar man all running after.

Next they came to a grocer's shop.
And the Elephant said to the Bad Baby, "Would you like a
chocolate biscuit?"
And the Bad Baby said, "Yes."
   So the Elephant stretched out his trunk and took a chocolate biscuit
for himself and a chocolate biscuit for the Bad Baby, and they went
rumpeta, rumpeta, rumpeta, all down the road, with the ice-cream
man, and the pork butcher, and the baker, and the snack bar man,
and the grocer all running after.

17

19

Next they came to a sweet shop.
And the Elephant said to the Bad Baby, "Would you like a lollipop?"
And the Bad Baby said, "Yes."

    So the Elephant stretched out his trunk and took a lollipop for himself and a lollipop for the Bad Baby, and they went rumpeta, rumpeta, rumpeta, all down the road, with the ice-cream man, and the pork butcher, and the baker, and the snack bar man, and the grocer, and the lady from the sweet shop all running after.

Next they came to a fruit barrow.
And the Elephant said to the Bad Baby, "Would you like an apple?"
And the Bad Baby said, "Yes."

    So the Elephant stretched out his trunk and took an apple for himself and an apple for the Bad Baby, and they went rumpeta, rumpeta, rumpeta, all down the road, with the ice-cream man, and the pork butcher, and the baker, and the snack bar man, and the grocer, and the lady from the sweet shop, and the barrow boy all running after.

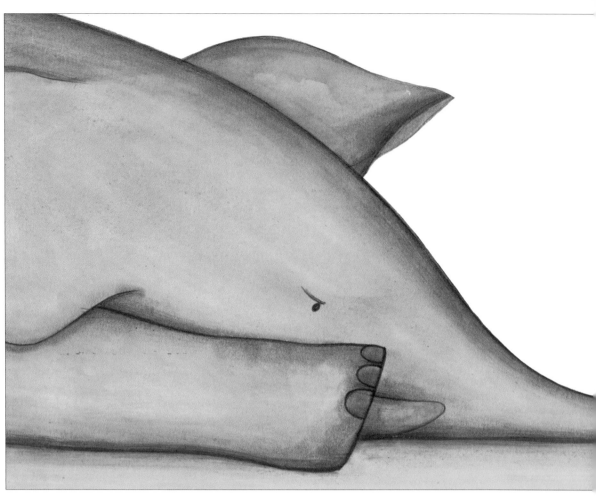

21

And the ice-cream man, and the pork butcher, and the baker, and the snack bar man, and the grocer, and the lady from the sweet shop, and the barrow boy all went BUMP into a heap.

23

Then the Elephant said to the Bad Baby, "But you haven't once said please!"
And then he said, "You haven't ONCE said please!"

Then the Elephant sat down suddenly in the middle of the road and the Bad Baby fell off.

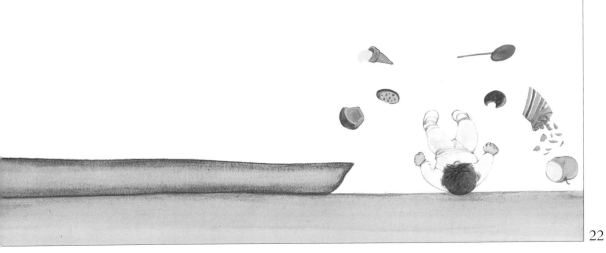

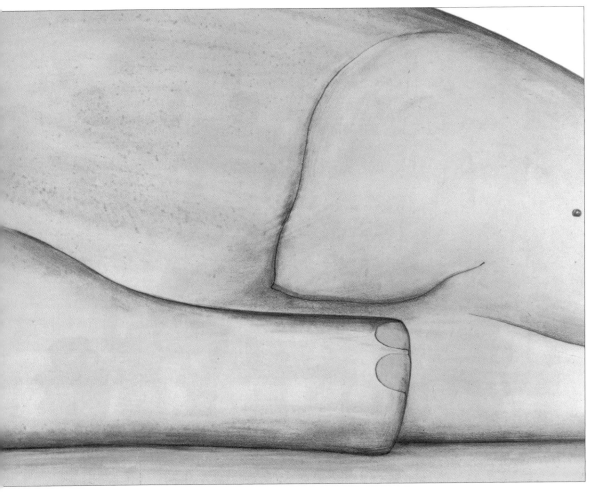

And the Elephant said, "But he never once said please!"

And the ice-cream man, and the pork butcher, and the baker, and the snack bar man, and the grocer, and the lady from the sweet shop, and the barrow boy all picked themselves up and said, "Just fancy that! He never *once* said please!"

And the Bad Baby said: "PLEASE! I want to go home to my Mummy!"

25

27

So the Elephant stretched out his trunk, and picked up the Bad Baby
and put him on his back, and they went rumpeta, rumpeta, rumpeta,
all down the road, with the ice-cream man, and the pork butcher, and
the baker, and the snack bar man, and the grocer, and the lady from
the sweet shop, and the barrow boy all running after.

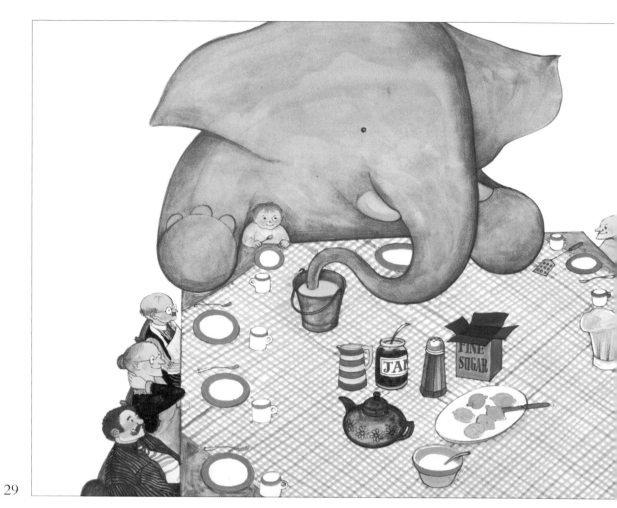

29

31

When the Bad Baby's Mummy saw them, she said, "Have you come for tea?"
And they all said, "Yes, *please!*"
So they all went in and had tea, and the Bad Baby's Mummy made pancakes for everybody.

Then the Elephant went rumpeta, rumpeta, rumpeta, all down the road, with the ice cream man, and the pork butcher, and the baker, and the snack bar man, and the grocer, and the lady from the sweet shop, and the barrow boy all running after.
And the Bad Baby went to bed.

A year after *The Elephant and the Bad Baby*, Briggs published another enduring picture book still popular with nursery classes more than thirty years later, this time with his own text. Playing with the story of Jack and the Beanstalk, *Jim and the Beanstalk* (1970) has a boy revisit the giant of the fairy tale, who has got old and laments having his treasures stolen from him by Jack. Jim helps him by having giant specs, false teeth and a wig made. The pictures are a cheerful mix of realism (townscapes, tea things, the giant's stubble) and caricature: people fall over and drop things in surprise. The book is popular in schools because it involves thinking about measuring (the giant's head), growing (the beanstalk), and scale (unusually big objects), as well as having a bit of a moral (better to help people than steal from them – or eat them on toast). But Briggs did not set out to draw a lesson. The story is characteristic of him in that it plays about with types of good and bad: the giant is not necessarily a villain, but he might still turn out to be dangerous. The boy is helpful but not endlessly patient: he looks bored when the giant reads to him from (a self-mocking touch) Raymond Briggs's nursery rhyme books *The White Land, Fee Fi Fo Fum* and *Ring-a-Ring o' Roses*. The book prefigures *The Man*, in which a sensitive and educated boy meets an older, rougher, demanding character whose needs he attends to. *The Man* reverses the size of the characters in *Jim and the Beanstalk*: in *The Man* it is the boy who is big. *The Man* also expanded upon the ideas hinted at in this picture book about difference and kindness.

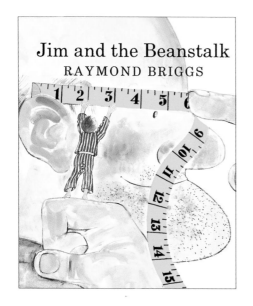

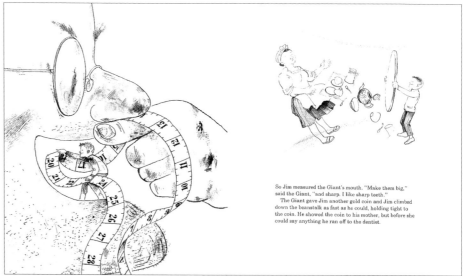

So Jim measured the Giant's mouth. "Make them big," said the Giant, "and sharp. I like sharp teeth."
The Giant gave Jim another gold coin and Jim climbed down the beanstalk as fast as he could, holding tight to the coin. He showed the coin to his mother, but before she could say anything he ran off to the dentist.

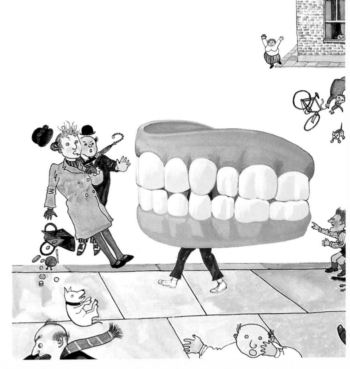

The dentist could hardly believe his eyes when he saw the giant gold coin, but he set to work straight away. He worked all night, and in the morning the teeth were ready.

Jim carried them home. Then he tied them on his back and climbed up the beanstalk.

The Giant loved his new teeth. He jumped up and down, champing his jaws and gnashing the teeth until the sparks flew.

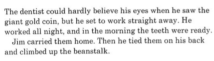

The Giant loved his glasses and began reading rhymes to Jim as soon as he put them on.

"You're a good boy," he said. "Now I can see you properly I wonder what you'd be like to eat? I can't eat anything much nowadays because I've got no teeth."

"Why don't you have false teeth?" asked Jim.

"False teeth!" roared the Giant. "Never heard of them!"

So Jim explained about false teeth while the Giant listened carefully.

"Get 'em!" said the Giant when Jim had finished. "Get 'em for me. I'll pay good gold."

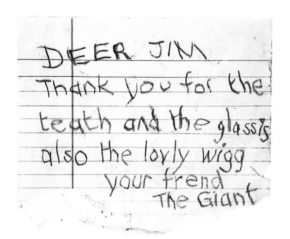

Above: note from the Giant to Jim at the end of
Jim and the Beanstalk
Below: note to the boy from the Man at the
end of *The Man*

The endings to the books echo each other. The giant sends Jim a misspelt thank-you note on a scrap of file paper signed 'your frend'. The Man leaves the boy a misspelt note on a scrap of file paper signed 'yor old mate'.

When *The Mother Goose Treasury* was published in 1966, Julia MacRae, then at the publisher, William Collins, wrote a fan letter to Richard Hough about the book. She said she envied him for being able to publish it. In 1967 she was headhunted by Hamish Hamilton and found herself working with the illustrator she had so admired. Author and editor first met at a lunch, both of them 'very nervous' about each other. It was the beginning of a productive collaboration that encompassed *Father Christmas, Fungus the Bogeyman, The Snowman, Gentleman Jim* and *When the Wind Blows*, before MacRae went her own way in 1979 to set up Julia MacRae Books. Briggs, loyal to his long-standing association with Hamish Hamilton, stayed with his publisher for *The Tin-Pot Foreign General and the Old Iron Woman* and the Wally books, but missed MacRae's editorial scrutiny and decided in 1991 to rejoin her. She edited *The Man* and *The Bear* before her retirement, and co-edited *Ethel and Ernest* afterwards.

MacRae was a skilled, careful and sensitive editor who erred on the side of restraint. There were some books and ideas that Briggs brought to her that got no further. Had she been his editor at the time, she would not, she says, have encouraged him to publish the Wally books. A lover of music, MacRae dislikes 'disharmony and ugliness' in any art form, and she tended to steer him away from grotesqueries. Being fearless and not easily shocked himself, Briggs could wander into territory that would 'make children's librarians throw up their hands in horror'. MacRae was the one who mediated between him and these hypothetical, shockable people, though at the same time she had 'total confidence in his integrity'.

The first book they assembled was, as it happened, a collection of stories put together by a librarian, Virginia Haviland, from the Library of Congress in Washington, *The Fairy Tale Treasury* (1972). Like *The Mother Goose Treasury*, it was a substantial task. Briggs illustrated thirty-two tales, with pictures (often half a dozen of them) on all 190 pages.

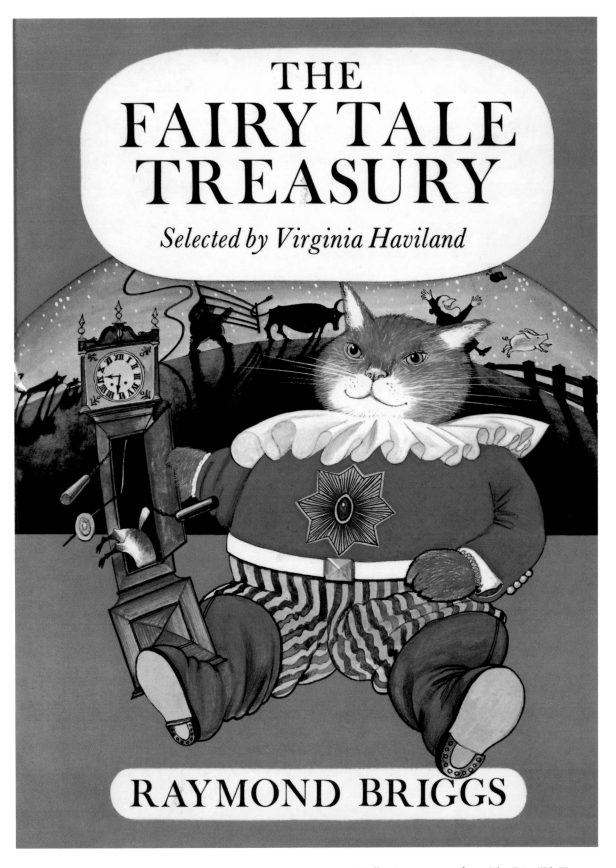

THE
FAIRY TALE
TREASURY

Selected by Virginia Haviland

RAYMOND BRIGGS

Following: extracts from *The Fairy Tale Treasury*

SARA CONE BRYANT

The Gingerbread Boy

Once upon a time there was a little old woman and a little old man, and they lived all alone in a little old house. They hadn't any little girls or any little boys, at all. So one day, the little old woman made a boy out of gingerbread; she made him a chocolate jacket, and put cinnamon seeds in it for buttons; his mouth was made of rose-coloured sugar; and he had a gay little cap of orange sugar-candy. When the little old woman had rolled him out, and dressed him up, and pinched his gingerbread shoes into shape, she put him in a pan; then she put the pan in the oven and shut the door; and she thought, "Now I shall have a little boy of my own."

When it was time for the Gingerbread Boy to be done she opened the oven door and pulled out the pan. Out jumped the Gingerbread Boy on to the floor, and away he ran, out of the door and down the street! The little old woman and the little old man ran after him as fast as they could, but he just laughed, and shouted –

"Run! run! as fast as you can!
"You can't catch me, I'm the Gingerbread Man!"
And they couldn't catch him.

The little Gingerbread Boy ran on and on, until he came to a cow, by the roadside. "Stop, little Gingerbread Boy," said the cow; "I want to eat you." The little Gingerbread Boy laughed, and said –

"I have run away from a little old woman,
"And a little old man,
"And I can run away from you, I can!"
"Run! run! as fast as you can!
"You can't catch me, I'm the Gingerbread Man!"
And the cow couldn't catch him.

The little Gingerbread Boy ran on, and on, and on, till he came to a horse, in the pasture. "Please stop, little Gingerbread Boy," said the horse, "you look very good to eat." But the little Gingerbread Boy laughed out loud. "Oho! Oho!" he said –

"I have run away from a little old woman,
"A little old man,
"A cow,
"And I can run away from you, I can!"

And, as the horse chased him, he looked over his shoulder and cried –

"Run! run! as fast as you can!
"You can't catch me, I'm the Gingerbread Man!"
And the horse couldn't catch him.

By and by the little Gingerbread Boy came to a barn full of threshers. When the threshers smelled the Gingerbread Boy, they tried to pick him up, and said, "Don't run so fast, little Gingerbread Boy, you look very good to eat." But the little Gingerbread Boy ran harder than ever, and as he ran he cried out –

"I have run away from a little old woman,
"A little old man,
"A cow,
"A horse,
"And I can run away from you, I can."

And when he found that he was ahead of the threshers, he turned and shouted back to them –

"Run! run! as fast as you can!

"You can't catch me, I'm the Gingerbread Man!"
And the threshers couldn't catch him.

Then the little Gingerbread Boy ran faster than ever. He ran and ran until he came to a field full of mowers. When the mowers saw how fine he looked, they ran after him, calling out, "Wait a bit! Wait a bit, little Gingerbread Boy, we wish to eat you!" But the little Gingerbread Boy laughed harder than ever, and ran like the wind. "Oho! oho!" he said –

"I have run away from a little old woman,
"A little old man,
"A cow,
"A horse,
"A barn full of threshers,
"And I can run away from you, I can!"

And when he found that he was ahead of the mowers, he turned and shouted back to them –

"Run! run! as fast as you can!
"You can't catch me, I'm the Gingerbread Man!"
And the mowers couldn't catch him.

By this time the little Gingerbread Boy was so proud that he didn't think anybody could catch him. Pretty soon he saw a fox coming across a field. The fox looked at him and began to run. But the little Gingerbread Boy shouted across to him, "You can't catch me!" The fox began to run faster, and the little Gingerbread Boy ran faster, and as he ran he chuckled –

"I have run away from a little old woman,
"A little old man,
"A cow,
"A horse,
"A barn full of threshers,
"A field full of mowers,
"And I can run away from you, I can!

"Run! run! as fast as you can!
"You can't catch me, I'm the Gingerbread Man!"
"Why," said the fox, "I would not catch you if I could. I would not think of disturbing you."

Just then, the little Gingerbread Boy came to a river. He could not swim across, and he wanted to keep running away from the cow and the horse and the people.

"Jump on my tail, and I will take you across," said the fox.

So the little Gingerbread Boy jumped on the fox's tail, and the fox swam into the river. When he was a little way from the shore he turned his head, and said, "You are too heavy on my tail, little Gingerbread Boy, I fear I shall let you get wet; jump on my back."

The little Gingerbread Boy jumped on his back.

A little farther out, the fox said, "I am afraid the water will cover you, there; jump on my shoulder."

The little Gingerbread Boy jumped on his shoulder.

In the middle of the stream the fox said, "Oh, dear! little Gingerbread Boy, my shoulder is sinking; jump on my nose, and I can hold you out of the water."

So the little Gingerbread Boy jumped on his nose.

The minute the fox got on to the shore he threw back his head, and gave a snap!

"Dear me!" said the little Gingerbread Boy, "I am a quarter gone!" The next minute he said, "Why, I am half gone!" The next minute he said, "My goodness gracious, I am three-quarters gone!"

And after that, the little Gingerbread Boy never said anything more at all.

JOSEPH JACOBS

The Story of the Three Little Pigs

Once upon a time when pigs spoke rhyme
And monkeys chewed tobacco,
And hens took snuff to make them tough,
And ducks went quack, quack, quack. O!

There was an old sow with three little pigs, and as she had not enough to keep them, she sent them out to seek their fortune. The first that went off met a man with a bundle of straw, and said to him:

"Please, man, give me that straw to build me a house."

Which the man did, and the little pig built a house with it. Presently came along a wolf, and knocked at the door, and said:

"Little pig, little pig, let me come in."

To which the pig answered:

"No, no, by the hair of my chiny chin chin."

The wolf then answered to that:

"Then I'll huff, and I'll puff, and I'll blow your house in."

So he huffed, and he puffed, and he blew his house in, and ate up the little pig.

The second little pig met a man with a bundle of furze and said:

"Please, man, give me that furze to build a house."

Which the man did, and the pig built his house. Then along came the wolf, and said:

22

"Little pig, little pig, let me come in."

"No, no, by the hair of my chiny chin chin."

"Then I'll huff, and I'll puff, and I'll blow your house in."

So he huffed, and he puffed, and he puffed, and he huffed, and at last he blew the house down, and he ate up the little pig.

The third little pig met a man with a load of bricks, and said:

"Please, man, give me those bricks to build a house with."

So the man gave him the bricks, and he built his house with them. So the wolf came, as he did to the other little pigs, and said:

"Little pig, little pig, let me come in."

"No, no, by the hair on my chiny chin chin."

"Then I'll huff, and I'll puff, and I'll blow your house in."

Well, he huffed, and he puffed, and he huffed and he puffed, and he puffed and huffed; but he could *not* get the house down. When he found that he could not, with all his huffing and puffing, blow the house down, he said:

"Little pig, I know where there is a nice field of turnips."

"Where?" said the little pig.

"Oh, in Mr. Smith's Home-field, and if you will be ready tomorrow morning I will call for you, and we will go together, and get some for dinner."

"Very well," said the little pig, "I will be ready. What time do you mean to go?"

"Oh, at six o'clock."

Well, the little pig got up at five, and got the turnips before the wolf came (which he did about six), who said:

"Little pig, are you ready?"

The little pig said: "Ready! I have been and come back again, and got a nice potful for dinner."

The wolf felt very angry at this, but thought that he could outwit the little pig somehow or other, so he said:

"Little pig, I know where there is a nice apple tree."

"Where?" said the pig.

"Down at Merry-Garden," replied the wolf, "and if you will not deceive me I will come for you at five o'clock tomorrow and get some apples."

Well, the little pig bustled up the next morning at four o'clock, and went off for the apples, hoping to get back before the wolf came; but he had farther to go, and had to climb the tree, so that just as he was coming down from it, he saw the wolf coming, which, as you may suppose, frightened him very much. When the wolf came up he said:

"Little pig, what! Are you here before me? Are they nice apples?"

"Yes, very," said the little pig. "I will throw you down one." And he threw it so far, that while the wolf went to pick it up, the little pig jumped down and ran home. The next day the wolf came again, and said to the little pig:

"Little pig, there is a fair at Shanklin this afternoon, will you go?"

"Oh yes," said the pig, "I will go; what time shall you be ready?"

"At three," said the wolf. So the little pig went off before the time as usual, and got to the fair, and bought a butter-churn, which he was going home with, when he saw the wolf coming. Now he could not tell what to do. So he got into the churn to hide, and by so doing turned it round, and it rolled down the hill with the pig in it, which frightened the wolf so much, that he ran home without going to the fair. He went to the little pig's house and

told him how frightened he had been by a great round thing which came down the hill past him. Then the little pig said:

"Hah, so I frightened you. I had been to the fair and bought a butter-churn, and when I saw you, I got into it, and rolled down the hill."

Then the wolf was very angry indeed, and declared he *would* eat up the little pig, and that he would get down the chimney after him. When the little pig saw what he was about, he filled his pot full of water, and made up a blazing fire. Just as the wolf was coming down, he took off the cover, and in fell the wolf. The little pig put the cover on again in an instant, boiled him up, and ate him for supper, and lived happy ever afterwards.

drank, and before a day was over he had drunk up the whole cellarfull. The Simpleton again asked for his bride, but the king was annoyed that a wretched fellow, called the Simpleton by everybody, should carry off his daughter, and so he made new conditions. He was to produce a man who could eat up a mountain of bread. The Simpleton did not hesitate long, but ran quickly off to the forest, and there in the same place sat a man who had fastened a strap round his body, making a very piteous face, and saying,

"I have eaten a whole bakehouse full of rolls, but what is the use of that when one is so hungry as I am? My stomach feels quite empty, and I am obliged to strap myself together, that I may not die of hunger."

The Simpleton was quite glad of this, and said,

"Get up quickly, and come along with me, and you shall have enough to eat."

THE BROTHERS GRIMM

The Elves and the Shoemaker

There was once a shoemaker who, through no fault of his own, had become poor. Finally he had leather enough left to make only one more pair of shoes.

One night he cut out the shoes which he would sew the next morning. Then he lay down, said his prayers, and fell asleep.

In the morning, after he had said his prayers and was ready to sit down to work, he found a fine pair of shoes standing finished on his table. He was so astonished he did not know what to think!

He took the shoes in his hand to examine them closely. They were beautifully polished, and so neatly sewn that not one stitch was out of place. They were as good as the work of a master shoemaker.

Soon a customer came in. He was so pleased with the shoes that he paid much more than the usual price for them. Now the shoemaker had enough money to buy leather for two more pairs of shoes.

The shoemaker cut these out that evening. The next day, full of fresh courage, he was about to go to work. But he did not need to – for when he got to his table, he found the shoes finished!

Buyers were not lacking for these shoes, either. The shoemaker received so much money that he was able to buy leather for four pairs of shoes this time.

118

Both the nursery rhyme and the fairy tale treasuries were remarkable for the variety of Briggs's drawing styles. It is rare now to find a volume by one illustrator in which the pictures are not obviously by the one hand. *The Fairy Tale Treasury* looks as if it could be the work of many. There are naturalistic animal drawings, caricatures, silhouettes, comic strip sequences that anticipate Briggs's later work; pictures in the style of Japanese prints, loose impressionistic sketches and satirical work of sharp clarity. Sometimes even within one story the styles contrast: the emperor in *The Emperor's New Clothes* parades nude, with his entourage, in a Beardsleyesque rococo line, while the crowd that guffaws does so with the simplification of a *Punch* cartoon. *The Fairy Tale Treasury* is a book of fertile inventiveness that shows the range of what Briggs could do, but it also shows an illustrator still searching for his style.

himself, and both the swindlers raised one arm in the air, as if they were holding something, and said: "See, these are the trousers, this is the coat, here is the mantle!" and so on. "It is as light as a spider's web. One might think one had nothing on, but that is the very beauty of it!"

"Yes!" said all the courtiers, but they could not see anything, for there was nothing to see.

"Will Your Imperial Majesty be graciously pleased to take off your clothes," said the impostors, "so that we may put on the new ones, along here before the great mirror."

The emperor took off all his clothes, and the impostors pretended to give him one article of dress after the other, of the new ones which they had pretended to make. They pretended to fasten something round his waist and to tie on something; this was the train, and the emperor turned round and round in front of the mirror.

"How well His Majesty looks in the new clothes! How becoming they are," cried all the people round. "What a design, and what colours! They are most gorgeous robes!"

"The canopy is waiting outside which is to be carried over Your Majesty in the procession," said the master of ceremonies.

"Well, I am quite ready," said the emperor. "Don't the clothes fit well?" and then he turned round again in front of the mirror, so that he should seem to be looking at his grand things.

The chamberlains who were to carry the train stooped and pretended to lift it from the ground with both hands, and they walked along with their hands in the air. They dared not let it appear that they could not see anything.

Then the emperor walked along in the procession under the gorgeous canopy, and everybody in the streets and at the windows exclaimed. "How beautiful the emperor's new clothes are! What a splendid train! And they fit to perfection!" Nobody would let it appear that he could see nothing, for then he would not be fit for his post, or else he was a fool.

None of the emperor's clothes had been so successful before.

"But he has got nothing on," said a little child.

"Oh, listen to the innocent," said its father; and one person whispered to the other what the child had said. "He has nothing on; a child says he has nothing on!"

"But he has nothing on!" at last cried all the people.

The emperor writhed, for he knew it was true, but he thought "The procession must go on now," so he held himself stiffer than ever, and the chamberlains held up the invisible train.

The
Nursery
Classics

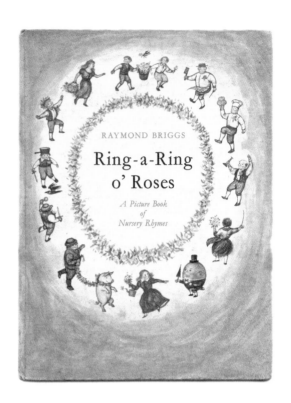

I N 1962 BRIGGS ILLUSTRATED his first picture book in colour. *Ring-a-Ring o' Roses: a Picture Book of Nursery Rhymes* combined full pages of watercolour and elaborately worked line drawings. Magical, skilled and pretty, these illustrations show Briggs's facility for marrying the fantastical and the realistic, as for instance in the fraught face of the old woman who lived in a shoe and the mischief the children in her care get up to (one child has tied up another in a giant shoelace). The watercolours in this book were reproduced with a misty softness which has an atmospheric effect; this prompted Briggs to use a sharper technique in his next collection of rhymes, *The White Land: a Picture Book of Traditional Rhymes and Verses* (1963), which was executed in gouache with a black line overlay. 'The printing in those days was much worse than today,' comments Briggs, tutting over an early edition of *The White Land* in which the line overlay was not quite synchronized with the colour. 'Now it's done in the Far East it's much better.' Considering one illustration in *The White Land* of a girl riding into the sea on a white horse, Briggs acknowledges a debt. 'That horse is from Victor Ambrus. I always pinch horses from him. He's the master of horse drawing.'

There is one small detail in the book that Briggs now perceives as a mistake. The book took its name from a riddle printed on the opening page that says: 'The land was white;/The seed was black;/It will take a good scholar/To riddle me that.' Underneath the rhyme Briggs drew the answer to the riddle: an open book. The pages are blank. 'I forgot to put the seeds in,' says Briggs. 'The point was that the seeds were the printed text.'

The White Land and a third collection of rhymes, *Fee Fi Fo Fum* (1964), demonstrated the comedy and quirkiness of interpretation that often makes Briggs's illustrations special. In *Fee Fi Fo Fum*, for instance, a king's banquet, illustrating 'Good King Arthur', includes an ailing nobleman who is not explicit in the text and has clearly eaten too much bag-pudding. When we are told of the Lion and the Unicorn that 'Some gave them white bread,/And some gave them brown;/Some gave them plum cake . . .' Briggs infers that they take tea together, so concluding their famous fight with a happy reconciliation. The Queen of Hearts is depicted as a playing card. None of these is the most obvious of illustrations: in each case the picture adds an idea to the text.

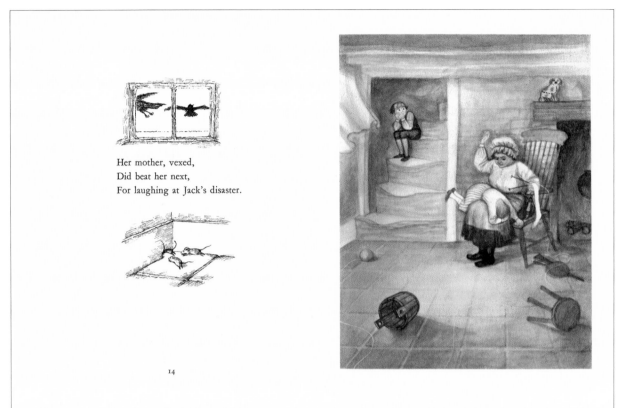

Her mother, vexed,
Did beat her next,
For laughing at Jack's disaster.

14

Many publishers today
would avoid choosing
this picture of a parent
smacking a child.

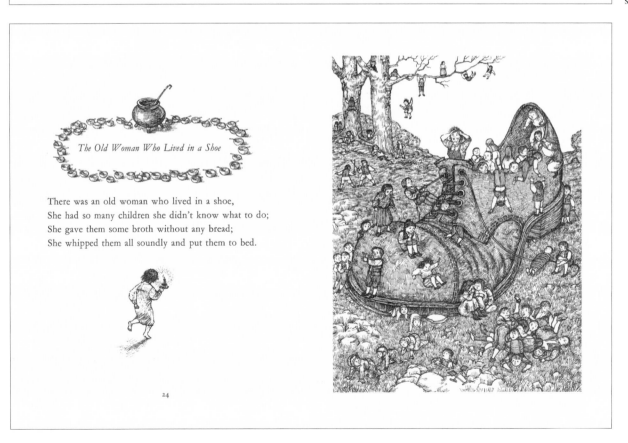

The Old Woman Who Lived in a Shoe

There was an old woman who lived in a shoe,
She had so many children she didn't know what to do;
She gave them some broth without any bread;
She whipped them all soundly and put them to bed.

24

From *Ring-a-Ring o' Roses*

A Picture Book of Traditional Rhymes & Verses

THE WHITE LAND

RAYMOND BRIGGS

My Mother Said

My mother said, I never should
Play with the gypsies in the wood.
If I did, then she would say:
Naughty girl to disobey
Your hair shan't curl and your shoes shan't shine,
You gypsy girl, you shan't be mine.
And my father said that if I did,
He'd rap my head with the teapot lid.

My mother said that I never should
Play with the gypsies in the wood.
The wood was dark, the grass was green;
By came Sally with a tambourine.
I went to sea—no ship to get across;
I paid ten shillings for a blind white horse.
I upped on his back and was off in a crack,
Sally tell my mother I shall never come back.

38

39

From *The White Land*

Good King Arthur

When good King Arthur ruled this land,
    He was a goodly King;
He stole three pecks of barley-meal
    To make a bag-pudding.

A bag-pudding the King did make,
    And stuffed it well with plums,
And in it put great lumps of fat,
    As big as my two thumbs.

8

The King and Queen did eat thereof,
    And noblemen beside;
And what they could not eat that night,
    The Queen next morning fried.

The Lion and the Unicorn

The lion and the unicorn
    Were fighting for the crown;
The lion beat the unicorn
    All round the town.

Some gave them white bread,
    And some gave them brown;
Some gave them plum cake
    And drummed them out of town.

15

The Queen of Hearts
  She made some tarts,
All on a summer's day;

The Queen of Hearts

The Knave of Hearts
He stole those tarts,

The King of Hearts
Called for the tarts,

And took them clean away.

And beat the Knave full sore;

The Knave of Hearts
  Brought back the tarts,
And vowed he'd steal no more.

16

17

55

From *Fee Fi Fo Fum*

THREE MEN IN A TUB
Rub-a-dub-dub,
Three men in a tub,
And how do you think they got there?
The butcher, the baker,
The candlestick-maker,
They all jumped out of a rotten
    potato,
'Twas enough to make a man stare.

PAT-A-CAKE
Pat-a-cake, pat-a-cake, baker's man,
Bake me a cake as fast as you can;
Pat it and prick it, and mark it with T,
Put it in the oven for Tommy and me.

This page and opposite: extracts from
The Mother Goose Treasury

Briggs enjoyed nursery rhymes as he did fairy tales, not least because they seemed to him to be about all of life, the everyday as well as our dreams and fears. Alice Torrey, editor at Briggs's US publisher, Coward McCann, was much taken with his three collections of rhymes. She suggested the co-publication of 'the biggest nursery rhyme book ever'. The result was *The Mother Goose Treasury* (1966), which had 800 illustrations, took Briggs eighteen months to complete, and won him his first Kate Greenaway Medal. The rhymes were sourced from *The Oxford Nursery Rhyme Book*, the classic compilation by Iona and Peter Opie.

The book was a huge task, not least because, unlike today when designers have a hand in picture books, Briggs was himself responsible for the layout of all 224 large-format pages. The design, he thinks now, is consequently 'very loose and rather messy. I just stuck the rhymes down and drew round them'. The book is a wealth of comic invention, sometimes wild, sometimes contemplative, sometimes literal, often unexpected, unpacking all the violence, humour, oddity and sweetness contained in nursery rhymes. Towards the end, says Briggs, as he felt increasingly overwhelmed by the volume of work, the pictures 'get more frenzied'. This image, below, in the last ten pages has a red-faced figure breathing fire, with steam coming out of his ears. Briggs now calls it 'rather rough and over the top', but, he says, 'That's exactly how I felt.'

AT BRILL
At Brill on the hill
The wind blows shrill,
The cook no meat can dress;
At Stow-on-the-Wold
The wind blows cold,
I know no more than this.

NOTHING-AT-ALL
There was an old woman called Nothing-at-all,
Who lived in a dwelling exceedingly small;
A man stretched his mouth to its utmost extent,
And down at one gulp house and old woman went.

SQUABBLES
My little old man and I fell out,
How shall we bring this matter about?
Bring it about as well as you can,
And get you gone, you little old man!

SING JIGMIJOLE
Sing jigmijole, the pudding bowl,
The table and the frame;
My master he did cudgel me,
For kissing of my dame.

211

THE MAD MAN
There was a man, he went mad,
He jumped into a paper bag;
The paper bag was too narrow,
He jumped into a wheelbarrow;
The wheelbarrow took on fire,
He jumped into a cow byre;
The cow byre was too nasty,
He jumped into an apple pasty;
The apple pasty was too sweet,
He jumped into Chester-le-Street;
Chester-le-Street was full of stones,
He fell down and broke his bones.

From *The Mother Goose Treasury*

IF ALL THE WORLD

If all the world was paper,
 And all the sea was ink,
If all the trees were bread and cheese,
 What should we have to drink?

99

LONDON BRIDGE

London Bridge is broken down,
  Broken down, broken down,
London Bridge is broken down,
  My fair lady.

Build it up with wood and clay,
  Wood and clay, wood and clay,
Build it up with wood and clay,
  My fair lady.

Wood and clay will wash away,
  Wash away, wash away,
Wood and clay will wash away,
  My fair lady.

Build it up with bricks and mortar,
  Bricks and mortar, bricks and
    mortar,
Build it up with bricks and mortar,
  My fair lady.

Bricks and mortar will not stay,
  Will not stay, will not stay,
Bricks and mortar will not stay,
  My fair lady.

Build it up with iron and steel,
  Iron and steel, iron and steel,
Build it up with iron and steel,
  My fair lady.

Iron and steel will bend and bow,
  Bend and bow, bend and bow,
Iron and steel will bend and bow,
  My fair lady.

Build it up with silver and gold,
  Silver and gold, silver and gold,
Build it up with silver and gold,
  My fair lady.

Silver and gold will be stolen away,
  Stolen away, stolen away,
Silver and gold will be stolen away,
  My fair lady.

Set a man to watch all night,
  Watch all night, watch all night,
Set a man to watch all night,
  My fair lady.

Suppose the man should fall asleep,
  Fall asleep, fall asleep,
Suppose the man should fall asleep,
  My fair lady.

Give him a pipe to smoke all night,
  Smoke all night, smoke all night,
Give him a pipe to smoke all night,
  My fair lady.

126

From *The Mother Goose Treasury*

RAYMOND BRIGGS
Father Christmas

Father Christmas *(1973)*
Father Christmas goes on Holiday *(1975)*

By the time Raymond Briggs published *Father Christmas* he had already won a Kate Greenaway Medal for *The Mother Goose Treasury*, but this was the book that guaranteed his immortality. It is Briggs's favourite of his own picture books because of its connection with his father. Ernest Briggs was a milkman who, like Santa, had a delivery round in all weathers. When Briggs re-imagined Father Christmas, he put the emphasis on Father, and portrayed a working man who has to go out in the cold, and is glad to come back to his humble but cosy home. This was a far cry from the regal Santas enthroned in glittering palaces and the factory owners with a staff of elves who often appear in other people's representations. Briggs's was the first ever working-class Father Christmas.

From the premise of this connection, all the details followed. Father Christmas lives in a brick house furnished with 1930s austerity. He has a chamber pot and an outside lavatory. Neither his alarm clock nor his kettle is electric. His television has an aerial that sits on top. We can't see, but surely it is black and white. He has an art deco wireless (though there is also a transistor in the kitchen), an old-fashioned cooker, a copper water-heater above the bath, a coal-fired stove and an old-fashioned electric fire instead of central heating. He keeps hens for the eggs for his breakfast fry-up, and makes sandwiches with white sliced bread to take to work. He makes pots of loose leaf tea from a caddy and cocoa with hot milk. He also grumbles. This is partly a characteristic of Briggs's father, but it is also to some extent a self-portrait. Briggs says: 'My father always grumbled, but in a humorous way . . . I'm a bit the same. Always moaning, but not fundamentally as depressed as I sound. If I was, I would be dead long ago.'

Ernest Briggs makes a guest appearance in the book. Towards the end of his round, Father Christmas meets a cheery early-morning milkman, who asks him, 'Still at it, mate?' The milkman has Ernest's face, and the registration number of his float has his initials and date of birth: ERB 1900.

Ernest Briggs on his milk float

Father Christmas's delivery round takes him and his two graceful reindeer to Raymond Briggs's own house, near Ditchling in Sussex, the layout of which is accurately reproduced in the book, down to the picture window looking from the living room onto the back garden and the split stable door at the front. He also makes a delivery to the Edwardian terrace Briggs grew up in, which reappears in *Ethel and Ernest*, to an igloo, a lighthouse, a caravan, the Houses of Parliament and, in a grand double-page spread, to Buckingham Palace, which has a forecourt of textured snow using granular watercolour.

When Julia MacRae was in America to sell US rights in this book, one publisher asked that this image of the Palace should be changed to a picture of the White House. MacRae, who recognized that the whole point of this book was the particularity of its setting, in time and place, walked out of the door. When the book was published in America, by a different company, it was published as Briggs drew it.

Father Christmas's catch phrase in the book is the mild expletive 'blooming'. Even 'blooming' was too strong a word for the wife of a mid-Western Baptist minister who wrote to Briggs after publication to express her distress that Father Christmas uttered it, and furthermore that he was depicted 'performing an act of personal hygiene' (using the outside lavatory). She declared that Briggs should apologize to every child who read the book. The minister's wife's letter now hangs next to Briggs's own lavatory.

The minister's wife was fortunate there was nothing more shocking in the book. Julia MacRae, who had the habit of writing comments in pencil on the blank borders surrounding Briggs's originals, which were masked with white tape if the work was to be shown, once came across a group of giggling spectators examining one of his drawings at an exhibition. A piece of white tape had been removed, and when she looked closer she read, in her own handwriting, the note: 'Please Raymond, no full-frontal nudity for Father Christmas!'

Father Christmas

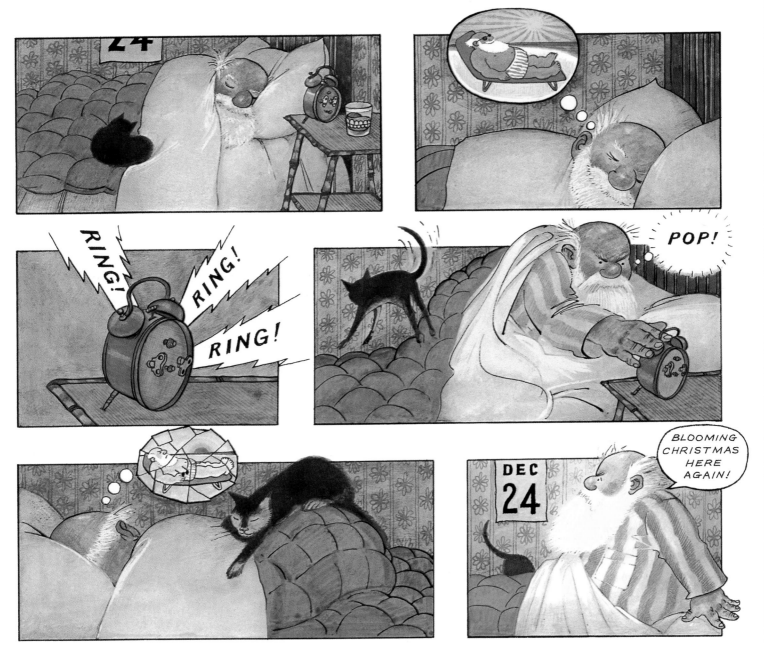

KEEP STILL YOU SILLY DEERS!

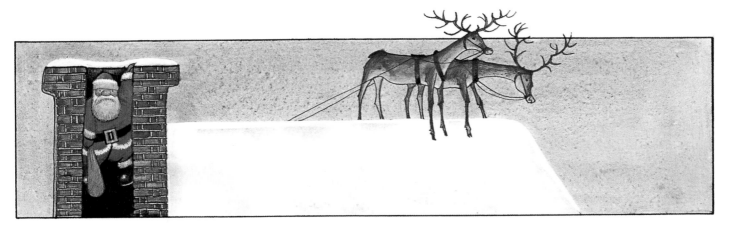

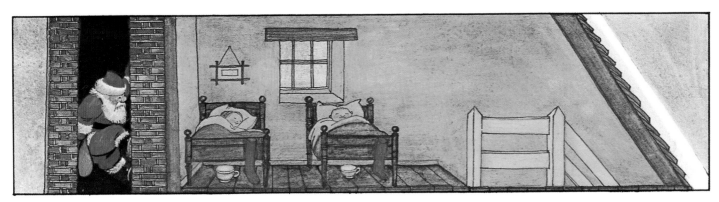

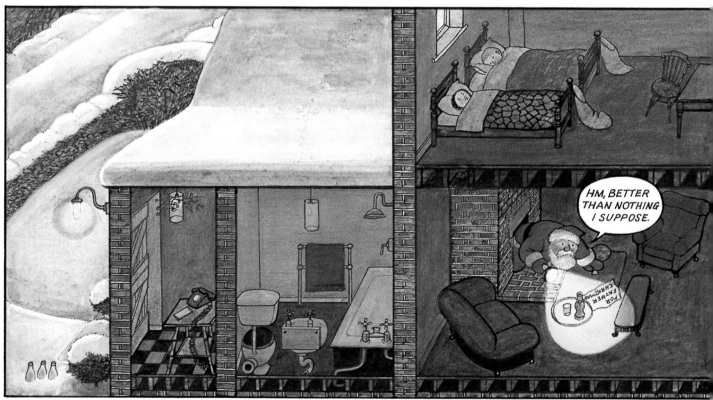

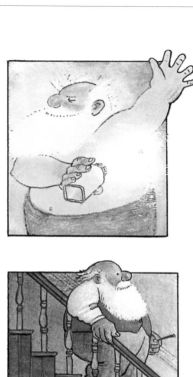

The End

One of the aspects of Father Christmas's character revealed by Briggs's pictures is that he loves to fantasize about holidays in the sun. The only pictures on his walls are posters of hot resorts – Majorca, Malta and Capri – and he relaxes by reading travel brochures. Briggs took this idea to its conclusion in his sequel, *Father Christmas goes on Holiday*.

Father Christmas potters in his vegetable garden and his greenhouse in early summer and plans his getaway. Before he wrote this book, Raymond Briggs's wife had died and he was invited away three times that summer to France, Scotland and then by his US publisher to attend the American Library Association Conference in Las Vegas. This became the itinerary for Father Christmas. He converts his sledge into a caravan, swots up on his French, sadly kennels his cat and dog (he is seen from the back using his hanky) and sets off. France offers rich food and a Van Gogh landscape, which he paints, but he gets an upset tum, misses cooked breakfasts, and disapproves of the drains. He moves on to Scotland, which has 'blooming marvellous' bagpipes, dancing (he joins in), whisky and haggis. But it's cold. He has a high old time in Las Vegas, gambling, swimming, basking in sunshine and luxury and running up big bills. Coming home, despite the backlog of post and weeds in the garden, is cause for celebration.

The real pleasure of this book, beyond the story, is in the skill and variety of the artwork. A full-page twilight over Las Vegas, the faces of French peasants and waiters and gamblers in an American casino, the scenery of Scotland, the spectacular scale of Nero's Palace, the patterns of a spotlit chorus line and shadowy nightclub audience, the seaside postcard quality of fat Father Christmas swimming in spotted trunks and the loving detail of his garden at home all contribute to the visual feast.

The political cartoonist Steve Bell remembers the impact *Father Christmas* had on him when he first saw it, long before he met the author. 'When I was a student I had an old friend who was also a cartoonist, and went to visit him in Brixton. He said, "Have you seen this?" and pulled out *Father Christmas*. I was completely bowled over. I thought, I want to do this. It showed you what could get published. It was not a traditional take on children's books. It was quite sour and

realistic. And it was funny and sad – a wistful take on things. I loved the way it was drawn, and the way it was written, and the fact that Father Christmas was a cantankerous old sod. It was such a new thing. I was delighted by that. It was a breath of new air.'

Film rights in *Father Christmas* were rashly sold in perpetuity by the publisher, at a time when film deals for picture books were rare. Now the usual arrangement is to sell an option lasting six months, after which, if production is not under way, rights revert. After John Coates made the film of *The Snowman*, he was eager also to animate *Father Christmas*, but was obliged to wait years to do so, while complicated and expensive negotiations bought the rights back.

Helped by the television screening of the animation, Briggs's *Father Christmas* achieved iconic status. The image of the patron saint of Christmas would never be the same again. Briggs created a landmark in his evolution, as did Coca-Cola (who first dressed him in red and white) and Clement C. Moore (who named his reindeer in *The Night Before Christmas*) before him. Thanks to Briggs, we will always now believe Father Christmas is a working man with quite a hard life.

It is remarkable that this comical character was created with such exuberance given the author's circumstances at the time. *Father Christmas* is dedicated to Briggs's parents, and the sequel to his wife Jean. All three died between the conception of the first and completion of the second of these two books.

Following: some extracts from *Father Christmas goes on Holiday*

Father Christmas goes on Holiday

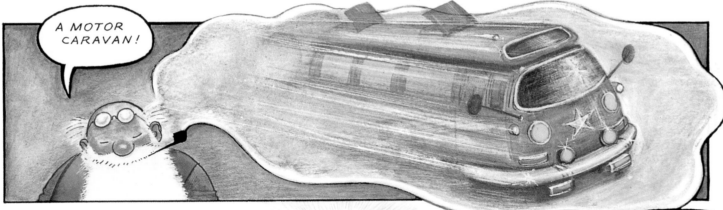

Father Christmas in France

Later, in Las Vegas

After a long night flight from Las Vegas…

The Snowman (1978)

After two years enmired in the slime and wordiness of *Fungus the Bogeyman* (see 'A Gallery of Characters', p.167), Raymond Briggs craved something pure, clean and wordless to work on. He woke one morning in a room filled with the light and silence of snow outside. That day a book was begun that went on to sell over two million copies in the US and UK alone in the twenty years after publication, and another character was born who has become a Christmas institution.

The nameless boy in the book also wakes to a snowy morning, and spends his day building a snowman in his garden, reluctant to leave it at bedtime. At midnight, he goes downstairs to visit his creation again. When he opens the front door, he sees the Snowman raise his hat. The boy and his magical friend play together in the house and the garage before they take off from the garden, hand in hand, into the sky. They fly to Brighton, the seaside resort near Briggs's home, and look out from the pier, until sunrise sends them home. The boy hugs his friend and goes back to bed. In the morning it is sunny and the Snowman has melted.

'People have told me that there is a flying snowman in the Rupert Bear comic strips. I probably would have stolen it if I'd known anything about it,' says Briggs, who is a fan of Rupert but missed this story. 'It just seemed to make sense for a snowman to fly up in the air, because snow flies down from the air.'

The Snowman is drawn and coloured in pencil crayon, which gives it a light, soft-focus quality compared to the gooier texture of *Fungus*'s watercolour. It develops with a perfectly readable logic, despite the complete absence of text, each frame imparting just as much information as is needed to further the story. Although the strip illustration resembles film, it has the advantage over film that it does not need to tell you everything. If one image shows the boy in his pyjamas looking out of the window at the snow and the next shows him pulling a sweater over his head, the reader infers the taking off of his pyjama top in between. So that when Briggs drew him putting on his trousers without drawing him putting on underpants, the underpants were implied between pictures. The animators, when the book was

made into a film, took this sequence literally, however, and decided the boy was in too much haste to go out in the snow to bother with underwear. It left generations of children preoccupied with the idea of his cold bottom.

The book was immediately a popular successor to *Father Christmas*. Its wordlessness meant that it worked for children of any age, and encouraged a happy interaction with parents. The story has a powerful appeal for children: the Snowman is an ideal companion because although he is big and cuddly like a father figure, he is playful and curious like a child, enjoying such simple pleasures as turning the light on and off, dressing up, playing with balloons and pretending to drive the car. And then, glory of glories, he takes you flying, as the strip cartoon pictures get bigger and open up with the vastness of the landscape into two double-page spreads of the snowy Downs and the Brighton Pavilion.

The Snowman, like most of Briggs's work, was drawn without models, with the exception of one page. For the sequence of twelve pictures of the boy asleep after his flying adventure, Briggs drew his partner's sleeping son, Tom. 'It's surprising how much people move in sleep and what a variety of positions they take up.'

The book has several Briggs trademarks. The boy's parents are portraits of his own; the setting is close to his home; the hero is an only child, as was Briggs; and the story ends in loss. Critics have seen, as Elaine Moss put it, 'intimations of mortality' in the way the story closes, 'having to confront the sadness of the thaw'. But Briggs offers a prosaic rather than a psychoanalytical explanation of the ending. 'If the central character goes away,' he says, 'it's always a useful way to end a book.' In this case it is also logical: snowmen do melt. With this fearless conclusion, Briggs lets children face the undiluted truth that things pass.

Logic dictates many of the details of the book. If the boy's friend is made of snow, it follows that he will be in danger from fireplaces and steam, bask in front of the fridge, like frozen food, be comfortable lying in the freezer, and take against images that suggest heat and sunshine: so he pulls a long face at a print of Van Gogh's *Sunflowers*.

The Snowman won the Victoria & Albert Museum's Francis Williams Award, a Boston Globe Horn Book Award (First Prize), a Dutch Silver Pen Award, and the Premio Critici in Erba in Italy. The film of the

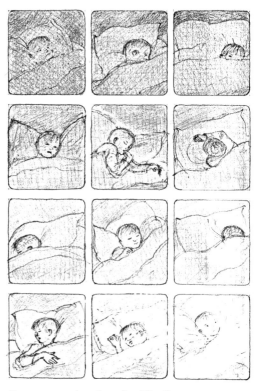

Preparatory drawings for *The Snowman*

book also won a BAFTA Award.

Briggs points out that his wintry story was not necessarily set at Christmas. In southern Britain, after all, snow before Christmas is rare. Again it was the film-makers who added a Christmas tree. Jeremy Isaacs of Channel Four commissioned John Coates of TVC to animate Briggs's book. The twenty-six-minute film, first broadcast in 1982, required considerably more material than the picture book – and so took the boy and the Snowman flying across the world to visit Father Christmas. Briggs's first reaction when he heard the news of this addition was that it sounded corny but he is pleased with the finished product, which he thinks perfectly good, not least because of the care with which each cel was coloured in the style of the book, using pencil crayons.

The Snowman is not inspired by Van Gogh's *Sunflowers*

Apart from the extended interpolations into the book, the animation made other alterations. The boy acquires a name, for instance, because one of the animators drew her son James's name on a Christmas parcel. In the film, the boy and the Snowman ride a motorbike through the countryside instead of merely sitting inside a stationary car. Father Christmas gives James a present of a snowman scarf, which consoles the boy when the Snowman has gone. The simple final frame of Briggs's book, in which the boy stands with his back to us beside the melted remains of his friend, placed in the isolating white of an otherwise empty page, is translated into a long shot in which the camera pulls back from the boy, leaving him kneeling, small and alone in the landscape.

Briggs was surprised that he has only received one letter of complaint from a reader who wanted to know why his book had missed out so much of the story of the film.

The American distributors were keen that a celebrity should introduce *The Snowman*. The pop star David Bowie was invited to do so, playing Briggs in a preamble to the film. Briggs remembers the 'awe-inspiring' day when Bowie came to record his contribution: he shook hands with everyone in a line, rather like the Queen, recorded his words, though not quite accurately as Briggs had written them, and left. Briggs was struck by his amazing, handsome face, with its 'weird, wolfy smile' and extraordinary eyes, 'quite different colours – one brown and one blue'.

Fritz Wegner illustration for *The Better Brown Stories* by Allan Ahlberg

The Snowman

RAYMOND BRIGGS

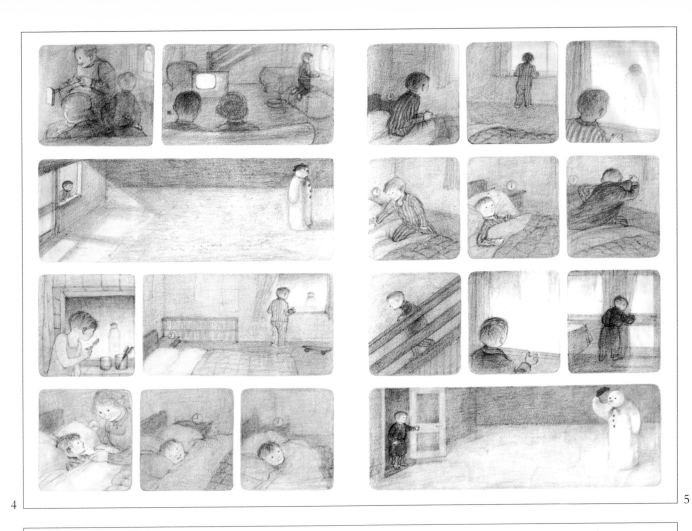

4

5

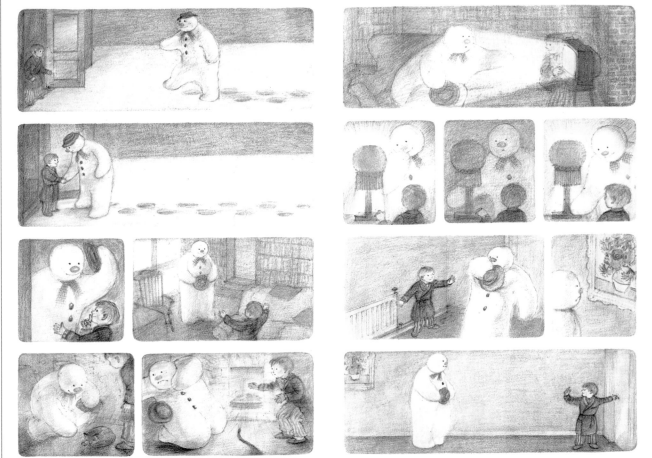

6

7

12

13

14

15

16

17

18

19

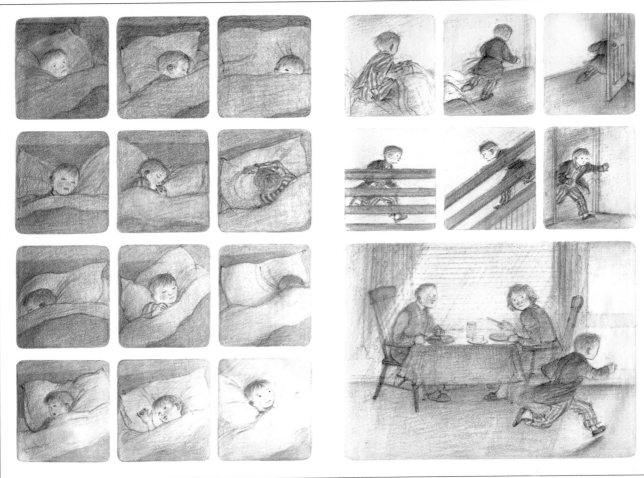

The animation has been shown on television at Christmas every year but one since 1982, and has been watched by an average of 2.8 million viewers a year. On video it has sold more than 2 million copies. Howard Blake's musical score included the song 'We're Walking in the Air', which became a hit for Welsh chorister Aled

Steve Bell cover illustration for *Private Eye*

Jones, who first sang the song for a Toys 'Я' Us TV advertisement but didn't sing for the film: Peter Auty's contribution was finally acknowledged when the credits were reshot in 2002. (When the film was first made, Auty had no agent to remind the film-makers, who forgot to credit him.) Faber sold over 250,000 copies of the sheet music. The song became so popular it experienced a backlash. When it reached number seven in the Top Ten of the Hate Parade, Briggs copied the list and faxed it gleefully to Howard Blake.

The wordless book gave rise to a text read on tape and CD by Bernard Cribbins. The film inspired two separate things: a ballet performed by the Scottish Ballet, and in 1999 a stage show by the Birmingham Repertory Theatre, which toured the country, and went on to Japan and the US. Over 70,000 people saw *The Snowman* show in its first two years, and it became a Christmas staple of Sadler's Wells. It is now in its fifth year. One of the features of the show is its reluctance to send young audiences away with Briggs's downbeat ending; its curtain call entails ten more scheduled minutes of exuberant dance by the company. There have been fourteen spin-off *Snowman* books, including the pop-up book, a short version (pointlessly) with text, and a how-to book of *Snowman* cross-stitch. Merchandise has included crockery, stationery, toys and puzzles, clothes, figurines, biscuits, jelly lollipops, and novelty ties with a musical chip. *The Snowman* has even been used to sell frozen chicken nuggets in Japan and air conditioning in VW Polos. He has featured in shopping centre grottoes around the country, and in the windows of Hamley's London toyshop in 1996. And he has been an inspiration to other cartoonists and illustrators.

Few Britons born in the last twenty years got through their childhood without encountering the Snowman. Briggs claims to have got 'bored to death' with him and reports that he torments others at Christmas by saying, 'We must watch it, it's part of the tradition.' To which everyone shouts, 'No!'

Snowman merchandise

Quotations from Briggs's preparatory note book for *The Bear*

The Bear (1994)

'Everyone has to do a bear book, sooner or later. It's compulsory,' says Briggs. The time had to come when he wrote his. With it he reverted to the soft pencil crayon of *The Snowman*, creating another nursery classic in a medium that expressed gentleness.

The huge bear that comes in one night through Tilly's bedroom window is the softest, whitest, shaggiest creature, and as Tilly says, 'He's the cuddliest thing in the whole world.' But, being a Briggs character, he is not just cuddly. He is also real and wild.

He has big black claws, and vast yellow teeth which he bares in what Tilly interprets as a yawn. Yet there is never a moment when the child is frightened, right from the beginning when he licks her awake with his big black tongue, and she says 'Hello, Bear' and invites him into bed. She is fearless in a way that her parents wouldn't be. This is a portrait of a competent, confident child that shows that children are copers. Just as Ug (the Boy Genius of the Stone Age) is cleverer than his parents, Tilly is braver. She is also Briggs's only female protagonist in a picture book.

There are echoes of other Briggs books in this. Like the Man, the Bear fulfils a childhood fantasy of having an amazing special friend, but again he turns out to be trouble to look after. Tilly gets cross at having to clear up the messes he makes, just as John gets annoyed at the Man's demands. As in *The Man* and *The Snowman*, the wonderful friend disappears, and leaves the child to grieve. But Tilly has something to comfort her that the boys in the two earlier books did not turn to: her mum and dad.

Tilly's relationship with her parents is one of the special things about this book. When she announces that a bear has come into her room, they respond kindly to what they see as her flight of fancy, and humour her about the creature throughout its stay, without ever believing in it. This gives rise to such memorable images as the picture of Tilly and her father snuggled up together and the father saying: 'Golly! Just imagine a great big bear in here now! I feel quite frightened.' And looming unseen behind the child and the father stands the enormous bear.

Goodnight, Tilly. Here's Teddy. He'll guard you and keep you safe all night.

He's a wise old bear, isn't he?

Yes, Teddy knows everything.

Goodnight, Mummy...

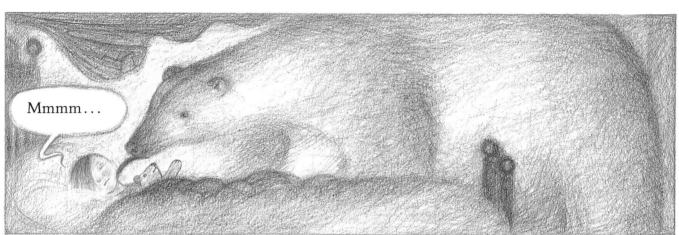

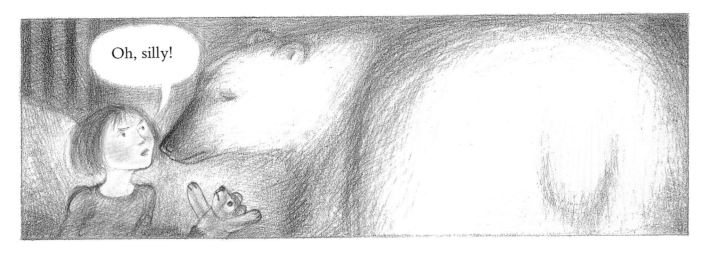

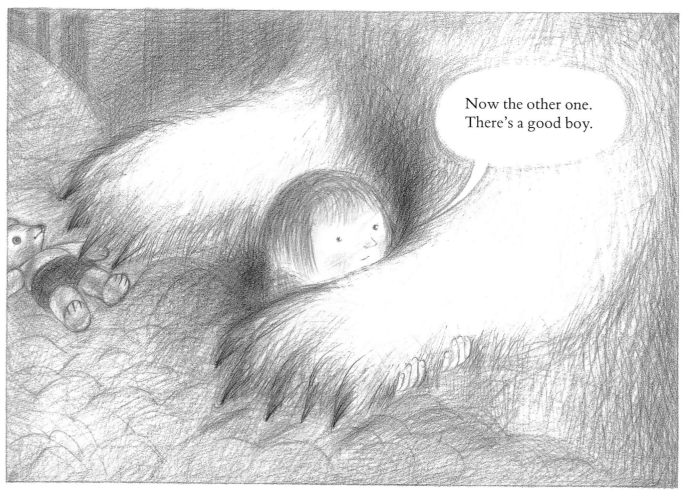

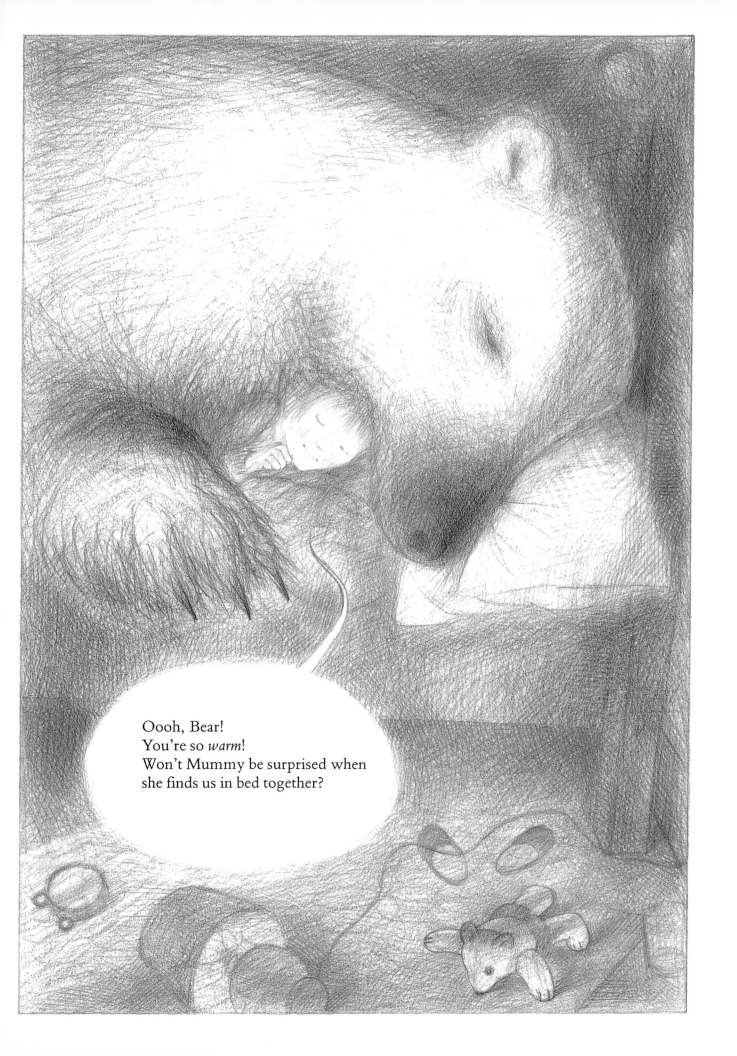

Oooh, Bear!
You're so *warm*!
Won't Mummy be surprised when
she finds us in bed together?

Mummy! Mummy! Daddy!
I was woken up by a bear!

Oh? What a surprise.
Was he a nice bear?

He licked my face with his tongue to wake me up.

Did he?

It was ever so rough.
And he had great big black wet nostrils
blowing hot air in my face.

Tilly! That's not very nice.

It's true!
He wanted to be friendly.

Well, mind you're friendly back.

You should see his teeth!
They're all yellow and enormous.
Longer than my fingers.
He's got real fangs.
I saw them when he yawned.
And his claws!
They're all black and curved like hooks.
He could easily tear me to bits
and eat me.

Tilly!
For goodness' sake!

He wouldn't though.
He really likes me. I can tell.

I'll take him up a bit
of bread and butter.

Aaah!
The wonderful world
of a child's imagination.

He's asleep now.
I've covered him up
with my duvet.

Did he like the bread
and butter?

He just licked it up with one flick.
You should see his tongue!
It's all black and about a foot long.

Ugh! Tilly!

Can he stay, Mummy?

Stay?
Yes, of course.
He can have
the spare bedroom.

No, I want him to sleep
with me.

Won't he roll over and squash
you in the night?

Oh?
What about me?

No, he'll just cuddle me.
I won't need a duvet.
He's the cuddliest thing
in the whole world.

You've got no *fur*, Daddy.
But you're *quite* nice.
I do still like you a *little* bit.

Oh, good.
I know I can't compete
with a bear.

Now you will be all right, won't you, Tilly?

Yes, Mummy.

Daddy is in his workshop,
but try not to bother him too often.

Yes, Mummy.
Don't fuss.
I've got the bear to guard me.

Yes, of course.
I really must dash.

Can I get extra milk from the milkman,
for the bear?

What?
Oh yes, of course.
Get as much as you like.
Byebye, Tilly.
Be good.

Byebye, Mummy.

You will make your bed, won't you?

I can't.
The bear is still in it.

Oh yes, well –
Never mind then –
Bye!

Hello, young lady.

Hello.
Can I have some extra
milk, please?
I've got a bear staying.

A bear, eh?
You'll need a lot
of extra milk
for a bear.
Is it a big bear?

Enormous.

Well . . .
Twenty pints, then?

I think one extra
will be sufficient,
thank you.

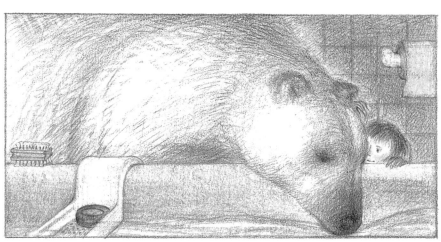

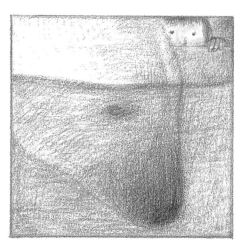

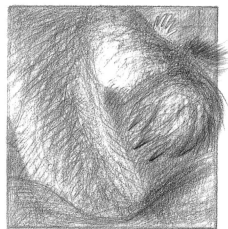

Is it true bears like honey?
Try some.
It's Daddy's very own.

My!
You are quick.
It's all gone.
You are a greedy pig, Bear.

Bear! Bear!

Where are you?

How can you disappear when you're so big?

OH NO!

What are you up to, Tilly?

The bear's done a poo. I'm burying it.

Oh, I see. Good girl.

Oh, there you are at last.
You're a very naughty bear,
making messes.

BAD
BOY!

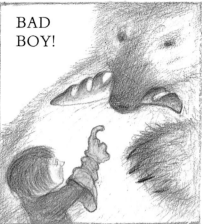

DON'T!

Now I've got to go
and wash again.
Don't disappear.
Wait here.

Oh, you BEAST!
You've weed on the floor!

Horrible! Horrible!
Horrible!

You are *awful*!
I *hate* you.
Don't you dare do it again.

I'm going upstairs to have
a long think about what to do
with you, Bear. So wait here.

Look, Bear, I've decided you and
I have got to have a serious talk.
Come and sit down properly.

Now listen.
You know Mummy said you could have
the spare bedroom?
Well, she's never once seen you
and she may change her mind when
she finds out how big you are.
And if you are going to do poos and wees
all over the house, she'll *never* let you stay.
Mummy and Daddy mustn't see you
or they might put you out.
Do you understand?

Will you pay attention
when I'm talking to you!

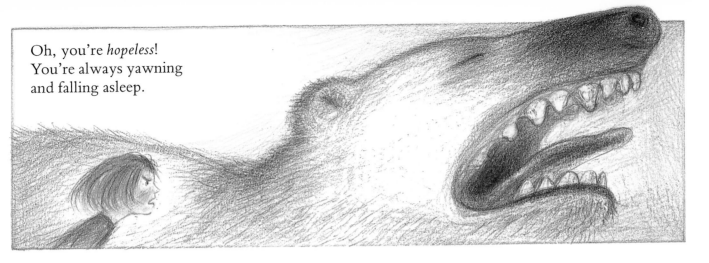

Oh, you're *hopeless*!
You're always yawning
and falling asleep.

WAKE UP!
WAKE UP!

Come with me, Bear.

I'm going to put you in the spare bedroom.

No! *Left* here, stupid.

Up the stairs you go. Giddy up!

Now, you can *hide* in there, but remember you're going to sleep with me.

NO! Not in here! It's Mummy and Daddy's bedroom.

Bear! Bear! You can't hide *there*!

Oh, you silly bear! You'll get such a ticking off!

Hello, Tilly!
Like something to eat?

Yes, please, I'm starving.
The bear is a lot of work, Daddy.

Is he settling in?

Yes, he's fast asleep in your bed.

Oh, good.
Will he sleep in between me and Mummy?

No. He's going to sleep with me.
You mustn't go in, you'll wake him up.

All right.
I'll go about on tiptoe
and we'll talk in whispers.

Hello,
Tilly!

Mummy!

Have you been all right?
Has the bear been looking
after you?

Sssh!

What?

Sssh! He's asleep.
In our bed.

Who is?

The bear. Sssh!
Mustn't go in
our bedroom.
Sssh!

Oh, I see.
Sssh!
We must whisper.

Yes. Sssh!

He's so big and quiet, Mummy.
He's the silentest thing I've ever known.
He's like a great big white ghost.

    Is he? He sounds like
    a polar bear.

I can't even hear him breathing
except when he cuddles me.
Then I can hear his heart beating,
too. His heart goes ever so slow –
it goes BOOM... ages ages ages
BOOM... ages ages ages BOOM,
like that.

    Well, I never. He's a long way
    from home, isn't he?

No, he's going to live here with me.
His fur is terrifically thick and
when I bury my nose in it,
it's ever so smelly, too.

    Oh Tilly, really!

No, it's a lovely smell.
All dark and smoky.

The bear is very good at hiding, Daddy.
Sometimes I look all over the house
and I can't find him.

But you say he is enormous?

He is, but he just seems to vanish like magic.
He could be in this room now
and you'd never know.

Golly!
Just imagine a great
big bear in here now!
I feel quite frightened.

Goodnight, darling.

Goodnight, Mummy.

Goodnight, Teddy.

There!

Now Tilly, whatever have you been
up to in our bedroom?

Oh, that wasn't me, Mummy.
That was the bear.

Well, the bear should have
tidied up, then.

I did tick him off.
I expect that's why he's hiding
under the bed. He's sulking.

Is he there now?

Yes, of course he is.

Shall I give him a
goodnight kiss, too?

No, better not.
I think he's asleep.

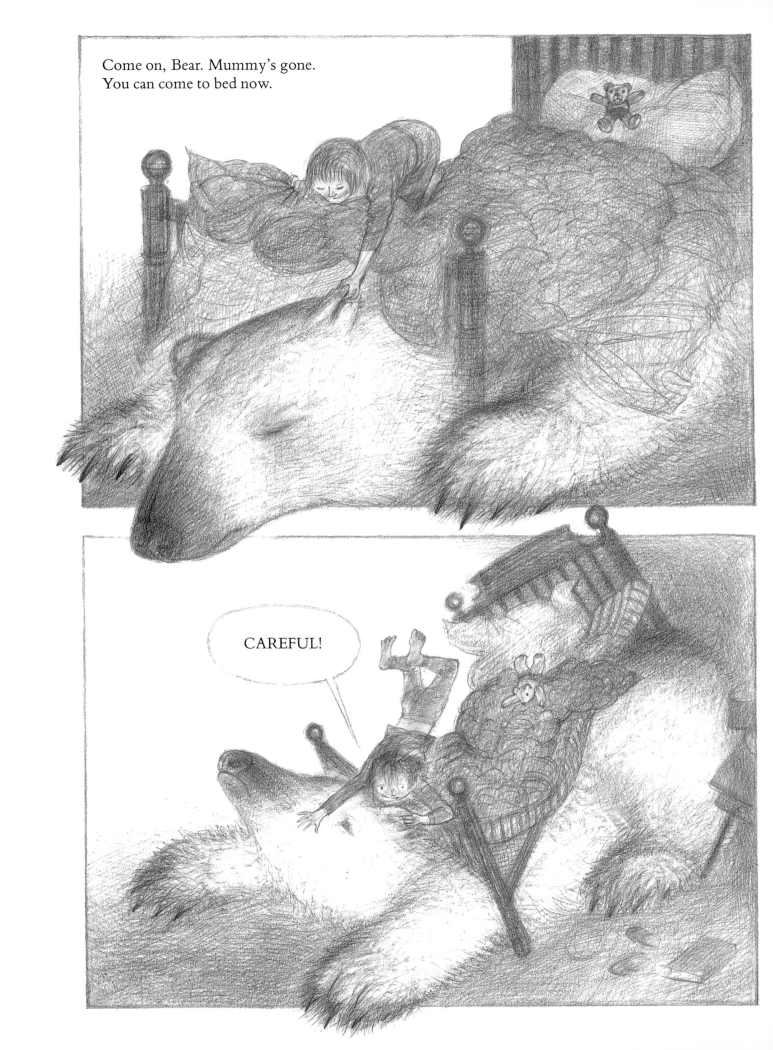

I love you,
Bear,

with all
my heart...

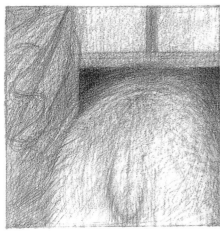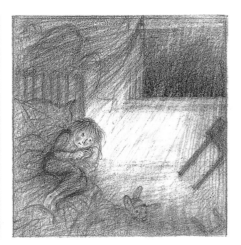

Tilly! Whatever's the matter?
He's gone!
He's gone!

Who?

The bear! He's gone!

Never mind, Tilly, sweetheart.
Don't cry, darling.
Bears can't live in houses
with people, can they, Teddy?
That sort of thing only
happens in story books.
Look Tilly, Teddy's nodding.
And he knows all
about bears,
don't you, Teddy?

Yes.
Teddy knows
everything.

The parents' incredulity raises the possibility that Tilly's bear might indeed be imaginary. But not for long. For the reader, as for Tilly, the bear is real, and the ending is confirmation. While the Snowman melts and the Man moves on to somewhere unknown, the Bear goes home to the frozen north and his own happy ending: another polar bear is seen in the final frame.

It was new to Briggs's books to have an inkling of what happened next to one of his magical characters. We also saw more of his arrival than usual: the bear appears as a distant tiny dot and comes closer and closer in a cinematic sequence that makes you hold your breath, as it becomes clear what kind of creature he is, and how huge. Movement from far to near is rare in Briggs's drawings: he usually draws, by his own admission, as if each scene were on a stage. Characters come in from the wings and perform, more or less, in two dimensions. He disapproves of the tendency of modern animation to make action constantly come at you. When it happens in Briggs's books, as here, or as in *Gentleman Jim*, with the opposite effect, when a police car recedes into the distance and becomes very small in a very large landscape, it is with a specific purpose. It expresses something important about scale.

The window through which the Bear enters is, though, a characteristic image. Fungus comes into human homes through the window (and is framed by one on the cover of the book). The Man does too. The boy sees the snow, and watches his snowman, through the window. Outside is a world of magic and strangeness or danger that may intrude into everyday experience through a window; inside is ordinary, everyday domesticity – safe and dull. When Briggs characters contemplate the enormities of the world, and the fearful things to face in it, they look out through the window, with their backs to us, as Jim does in *When the Wind Blows* when there are forces outside beyond his control that will destroy his domestic sanctuary, and as Wally does after his mother's funeral when he has to face the world alone.

The format of *The Bear* was unusual. The book was bigger than standard picture book size, and taller than most bookshelves. But this was the size that author and editor believed it had to be: the bear should be overwhelming, all-enveloping. Reading the book should feel like being embraced in a bear hug. Subsequent reproduction in smaller formats loses something.

The intense sensual presence of the Bear, who is so delightful to cuddle up with because he is so warm and soft and huge, triggered a small flare-up of critical anxiety, which equated sensuality with sexuality. The Bear was male, and a stranger, and Tilly invited him into bed. If any children who read the book find a polar bear filling their bedroom one morning, let's hope they will know better.

The Bear was yet another Briggs inspiration for a film: a Channel Four animation came out in 1996. It bypassed the dialogue of Briggs's book, and made another silent film, like *The Snowman*. Although he thought the film 'beautifully done', Briggs regretted that it did not make more use of the idea of a huge creature inside the house that the parents do not know about. 'It lost the humour and the tension as soon as they were outside the house. They had the Bear and the girl fly away into the sky together. I would have kept them in the house and then had a climactic moment when the parents do discover the Bear, and the girl pacifies them, and tells them it's all right, it's just a huge bear. That would have been my film. But that's the thing about films of your books: it's not what you would have done.'

A birthday card for Julia MacRae

The Adventures of Bert (2001)
A Bit More Bert (2002)

Twenty-eight years after he last illustrated a book by another author, Briggs accepted an invitation to collaborate. 'Usually there is no point in illustrating a text by someone else when you can do your own,' says Briggs, laconically. 'Besides, you're then working for half pay.'

If their own comical dialogue, used for publicity, is to be believed (and it isn't), Briggs and Ahlberg agreed to work together because Ahlberg 'needed an illustrator ... and Quentin Blake was busy, and

Meet Bert.
This is him.
Say hallo to Bert.

Hallo!

Helen Oxenbury was busy and Michael Foreman and Shirley Hughes, and he thought, well, there's poor old Raymond Briggs there, all on his own down in Sussex.' Briggs claimed that he thought that 'Ahlberg, with his funny foreign name, was one of these asylum-seeker johnnies and that was how he had ended up at Penguin. I'd never heard of him. I thought Penguin wanted to put him alongside someone like me to give the poor devil a start in life.'

In fact, of course, the collaboration was born of a huge mutual respect. Ahlberg wrote two books for very young readers with a few words whose simplicity is deceptive. They star Bert, an optimistic innocent to whom unfortunate things happen, such as getting a shirt stuck on his head which makes him fall downstairs, into the

Meet Mrs Bert.
This is her.
Say hallo to her
as well.

Hallo!

Meet Baby Bert.
Don't say hallo to him.
He is fast asleep.

Shh!
Turn the page . . . quietly.

street and onto the back of a lorry which takes him to Scotland, so
he has to hitchhike home in the rain. With splendid silliness, all of
Bert's family, associates, acquaintances and pets are also called Bert.
His adventures are full of things that seem similarly surreal but turn
out to be logical: a barking cardboard box contains a dog; a sausage
that chases Bert down the street is a man in a promotional sausage
costume. (In this respect Bert is like the hero of Ahlberg's *The Man
Who Wore All His Clothes*, who bizarrely goes to work wearing his
entire wardrobe but turns out in the end to have a job as a
department store Santa, for which he needs a lot of padding.)

Briggs interpreted Bert, who is a husband and father but has the
naïveté of a toddler, as an overgrown child. He looks boyish but

Oh no!
Now look what you've done.

rotund, or as one reviewer put it, 'the Snowman reborn as a rugby player'. Both Bert's wife, Mrs Bert, and his mother, Grandma Bert (in *A Bit More Bert*), revert to the dumpy Briggsian type that recalls his own mother, all flowery pinnies and curly perms. The pictures are clear and easy to interpret, and use full pages, spreads and comic strip boxes to vary the pace. They insert visual jokes, such as the striped tail that emerges from a margin although readers never see the rest of the cat. They are cheerful, like Bert, with emotive moments, such as Bert's reunion with his lost dog (called Bert). Like the text, the illustrations are subtler than is instantly apparent: townscapes, rainy countryside and twilights add atmosphere, and both text and pictures play with crossing the fourth wall. One of

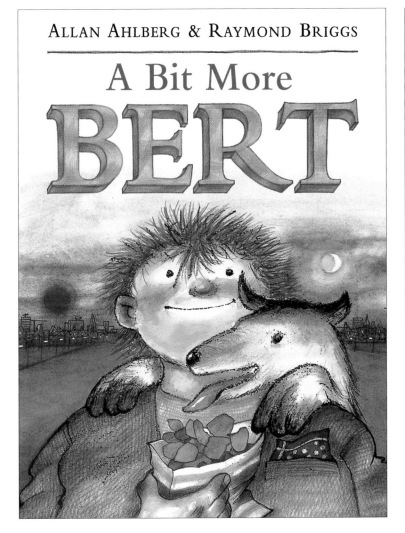

ALLAN AHLBERG & RAYMOND BRIGGS

A Bit More
BERT

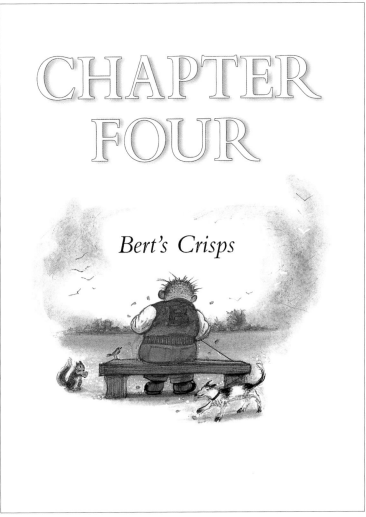

CHAPTER
FOUR

Bert's Crisps

the strengths of these books is that they are interactive: they involve small children in waving, talking to the characters and hushing up so as not to wake the baby. The book makes them fail at this last, and get into trouble. Reviewer Kate Kellaway pointed out: 'Little children – don't ask me why – always find mock reproof from adults killingly funny. Ahlberg and Briggs understand this, and that is just the beginning of what they know.'

The Bert stories were originally conceived by author and illustrator as small books, and it is still evident that this might have been their ideal format. Instead, the books were published in a size to suit, not the wishes of the author and illustrator, but their reputations. Briggs says: 'In publishing today creative decisions are

Bert is hungry.
He wants a bag of crisps.
Which flavour should he get?

Bert shares his crisps.
One for Mrs Bert.

One for
Grandma Bert.

One for
Baby Bert.

One for
Bert the dog . . .   and one for you!

no longer made by creative people. The experts said, "Small books don't sell." When I mentioned *Thomas the Tank Engine*, *Mr Men*, Beatrix Potter, they went all red and looked down at their boots.' Nevertheless, critics responded enthusiastically: 'structured like a perfectly timed joke', 'brilliant stuff', 'simple tales that unleash great ponderings, like Bert's role in the universe'. They liked the slapstick and the drolleries, in both text and pictures. Briggs and Ahlberg enjoy each other's humour, and it shows.

A Gallery of Characters

FUNGAS THE
BOGEY MAN

FATHER
CHRISTMAS

THE
SNOWMAN

THE
MAN

JAMES
FROM
WHEN THE
WIND
BLOWS

HILDA
FROM
WHEN THE
WIND
BLOWS

THE BOY
FROM
THE SNOW
MAN

RAYMOND BRIGGS
CHARECTERS

1. Fungus
2. Gentleman Jim
3. Wally
Previous page: illustration by
Ryan Vincent, age eleven. Sent
to Raymond Briggs in 1995

RAYMOND BRIGGS'S characters are remarkably various. And yet there is common ground between Fungus the Bogeyman, who lives underground and revels in muck, Gentleman Jim, the lavatory cleaner who aspires to a more exciting life, Unlucky Wally, who is pimply and unattractive and unsuccessful, the Man, the miniature vagrant who shows up in the bedroom of a middle-class boy, and Ug, the Stone Age boy who hankers for something softer to wear than his stone trousers.

It is not only that all these characters speak to an adult audience. Nor only that (with the exception of Wally, who is not drawn as a cartoon strip) they all demonstrate why, as Briggs vehemently believes, comic strips should be generally thought of as a subtle and expressive literary and visual form, as they are elsewhere in Europe. There is a self-referential joke in *Fungus the Bogeyman* in which Briggs glosses 'strip cartoons' as 'a form of entertainment for the simple-minded', even as he is in the process of refuting this definition.

Certain themes recur in all these books. A Briggs hero is always limited by his background and circumstances, but has some unfulfillable inkling of greater possibilities. Fungus thinks for himself enough to wonder what the point of his job is: 'At least I'm good at engendering boils . . . but do the boils do any GOOD?' But he can only conclude hopelessly: 'Theirs not to reason why.' Jim the lavatory cleaner has no chance of making his life more interesting because he doesn't know enough to realize his dreams. He doesn't even understand that the adventure fiction that inspires those dreams is no kind of guide to reality. Wally is all too aware of his own, mostly physical, limitations, and buys chest expanders and tries to get tanned in order to improve his luck with women, but no one will ever really care about him apart from his parents. His nose-picking and his smelly feet will always sabotage his hopes. Ug has ideas beyond the narrowness of his upbringing and has left his parents behind. But it is characteristic of Briggs that these ideas go nowhere and Ug is no better off for having come up with them.

Even the most fantastical of these characters is not so different from us: inadequacy is a common experience. Briggs's view of the world is pessimistic but it is also humane. While he is preoccupied with the fact that life can turn out to be pretty disappointing, he still gives empathetic and poignant attention to the disappointed lives and the unrealized dreams. And then he gets as many jokes out of these lives as he can. The end of his stories may be tragic, but the substance of them is comic. Just like life, in other words.

Briggs once remarked: 'When a baby is born, people say: "Isn't it marvellous?" But the child may grow up to be a forty-one-year-old balding double-glazing salesman. No one says: "Oh how marvellous, so-and-so's just had a forty-one-year-old balding double-glazing salesman."' He can't help seeing a pathetic end in a promising beginning. Even Briggs's most playful books are infused with a sense of mortality. *Fungus* is particularly Beckettian ('born astride the grave'), as it reminds us that life is a process of decay. One of the book's epigraphs, from Herrick, spells it out: 'Putrefaction is the End/Of all that Nature doth entend.' Briggs has the rare talent of being able to produce a *memento mori* that is a laugh a minute.

Briggs characters are held back by being ill-equipped for the world. When *Ethel and Ernest* was published it seemed to be a kind of key to all these books, illustrating a theme they all touched upon: the gulf between education and a lack of it, as expressed in Briggs's own experience of moving into a world which his parents, for all their innate intelligence, did not really understand. Briggs explores the gap between generations, but also the gap between the aesthete and the anti-intellectual. In *The Man* it is particularly apparent that this is a class divide – between the working class that Briggs came from and the middle class that he grew into.

Another identifiable trait of Briggs's work is his homeliness and his delight in domestic settings. His characters never live anywhere grandiose; he has unheroic heroes whose idea of luxury is putting the kettle on. They are little people going about their little lives. When Briggs was an art student, he says, he was encouraged to give a great deal of attention to the masterpieces of the Italian Renaissance, but these were not his favourite pictures; he was turned off by their piety and melodrama. What he liked better were the pictures of the Northern Europeans, the Dutch and Flemish genre paintings. Brueghel, in particular. As soon as he says this, it is impossible not to see a connection between Briggs's small, round, homely figures and

4

5

6

4. The Man
5. Ug
6. Ethel and Ernest

165

Brueghel's peasants. Jim and Ug, the dumpy little Man and Fungus in his dungarees (with the emphasis on dung) are all this shape. And as in Brueghel's pictures, the figures are comical, but there is something dignified about them too. They are the stars of their own show.

Briggs describes how his characters come to be. 'Most of my ideas seem to be based on a simple premise. Let's assume that something imaginary – a snowman, a bogeyman, a Father Christmas – is wholly real, and then proceed logically from there. That's all there is to it. It's logic, not imagination.' Logic such as this nevertheless creates whole worlds. And Briggs has to imagine his ideas visually down to the last detail. Meanwhile the other driving force of the books is humour. Often if you ask Briggs why a particular page or frame was written or drawn as it is, he replies: 'I thought it was funny.' The joke is, in the end, all the *raison d'être* anyone needs.

Pieter Brueghel, Children's Games, 1560

From *Ug: Boy Genius of the Stone Age*

Fungus the Bogeyman (1977)

Raymond Briggs says that Fungus the Bogeyman looks like his mother. This is surprising, given that Fungus is green with a dorsal fin, webbed hands, hairy ears, horns and a Mohican. 'But Fungus has my mother's thin, wide mouth and wide nose,' says Briggs. He attributes the likeness to the power of a mother's face in a child's psyche: 'It's the first face you see, and the most important to you.' All artists know what it is to find a resemblance to their closest relations in their portraits of other people, but in fact there is more sense in a connection between Briggs's mother and his character than at first appears.

Fungus was invented, says Briggs, partly in reaction to the prissiness of children's books at the time. 'I wanted to show the petty nastiness of life – slime and spit and dandruff, all this awful stuff which is slightly funny because it detracts from human dignity and our pretensions.' Briggs, who himself has no obvious pretensions, has also always been attuned to that part of children that delights in the scatological and finds bodily functions fascinating and funny. The book is not, though, intended to upset polite society. He says, 'I wasn't trying to shock people.' In fact he did set his own limits, which seem to have been rather more constrained than the taste of the general public. 'I got lots of letters afterwards from people suggesting more ideas for Fungus, and some of them I thought, No, that's just disgusting. Everyone has a point on the scale of comic disgustingness when they turn off and find it unfunny. Even in Monty Python I turn off at the point where Cleese brings in his dead mother in a bin bag and there is talk of eating her.'

The book demonstrates the interesting truth, though, that a (harmless) revolting idea pursued to an extreme goes beyond revulsion. Once, discussing Monty Python's 'Mr Creosote' scene in *The Meaning of Life*, Briggs remarked that it is the excessive quantity of vomiting that makes the scene funny. If the obese diner had not thrown up for so long, it would have been merely unpleasant to watch. The unbridledness is what is unexpected and comic.

167

This same unbridled quality is true of *Fungus*. No popular work had ever progressed so far along the path of the playground fascination with all things yucky. Such excess arrives at a point when squeamishness gives way to fascination and admiration.

Even its critics recognized that the book goes beyond the 'yuck factor' to invent a complicated character with unexpected traits. Fungus is revolting but he is not horrific. The truly disgusting aspect of human beings and their civilization is not that they sweat and have pimples. As Briggs's complete body of work demonstrates, what should really dismay us is man's capacity for inhumanity to man. And Fungus is not cruel or violent. He is a pacifist. Bogey guns are made of wood. They make no noise, have no ammunition and do not fire, so they do no damage. Bogeymen, despite the boils on the back of the neck and the bumps in the night that they engender in the course of their work, are peculiarly sensitive and gentle. They are homeloving creatures who care for their families. The book reveals that 'Bogeymen are extremely quiet in their movements and in their voices . . . At home they are gentle, shy and very polite to one another.' So perhaps Briggs's mother's face is not so inappropriate after all.

There is also truth in the idea that *Fungus* is a book about love. Briggs said after it was published: 'I'm noticing that all my characters now are sad old men, or rather, sad middle-aged men, which is what

I am probably' (said laughingly). 'Life is sad really but there's also love, which makes life worth living. Fungus has a loving relationship with his wife, which makes it bearable.'

Fungus began as an idea for a children's alphabet in which each letter stood for something revolting ('S is for Spit, B is for Bottom,' Briggs explains). Some letters of this original alphabet survive in the book, on the wall of Fungus's son Mould's bedroom: A is for Apple (with worms in it), B is for Bog, C is for Cowpat . . .

Fungus has breakfast with his wife and son before setting off to work on his Bogeybike

Hear that, son? Mind you wrap up well or you'll get dry — Here Mildew, look. This milk's not solid yet — It's still white.

I must speak to that milkman.

OK Dad.

Bogey cows are thin, dismal-looking creatures. Hornless and tail-less, they graze on the yellowing grass in the muddy fields. Their watery milk is half-sour when it leaves the cow and by the time it has been delivered it is clotting and turning a pale green. This is how Bogeymen like it. All Bogey cows (and most other cows) are polygastric[1] poephagus[2] poleys[3].

BOGEY NEWSPAPERS
All Bogeys are misoneists (those who hate anything new.) Consequently, they do not like "news". They prefer "olds". All the information in Bogey oldspapers is guaranteed to be at least one year old. The older the information the more highly Bogeys value it.
However, Bogeys are usually too apathetic to take an interest in important events, no matter how old, so their oldspapers are filled with "strip cartoons" – (a form of entertainment for the simple-minded) which has a large and devoted following in Bogeydom, and "stick-ups". *
Bogey stick-ups present an interesting contrast to "pin-ups," as Bogeymen like their stick-ups to be pictures of fat, ugly, heavily-clothed, old Bogey women.
* stick-ups: pin-ups. Bogey newspapers are so wet, and Bogey walls so mucky, no pins are needed.

Sully Sloven: (88-93-99) Grey-haired Sully is 84. Her favourite colour is bile green and her favourite pets are her twenty-seven sewer-rats.

LATER

Oooh! What a lovely egg, drear! Really ripe and fuscous * Mmmm, the smell!

Well, I'd better be off, Mildew my love.

Take care, Fungus my darkling. Try not to get your feet dry.

Give us a nice slimy kiss, drear.

* fuscous: brown tinged with black or grey

* Boibye, Sourheart. Boibye, Fungus love....

SMELL THIS HOUSE

Boibye Mould.

I'll glaur* the bar muffs on the Bogeybike, Dad.

* Boibye: corruption of "Boils be with you"

*glaur : to make muddy

171

1 polygastric : having many stomachs   2 poephagus : subsisting on grass   3 poleys : hornless (of cattle)

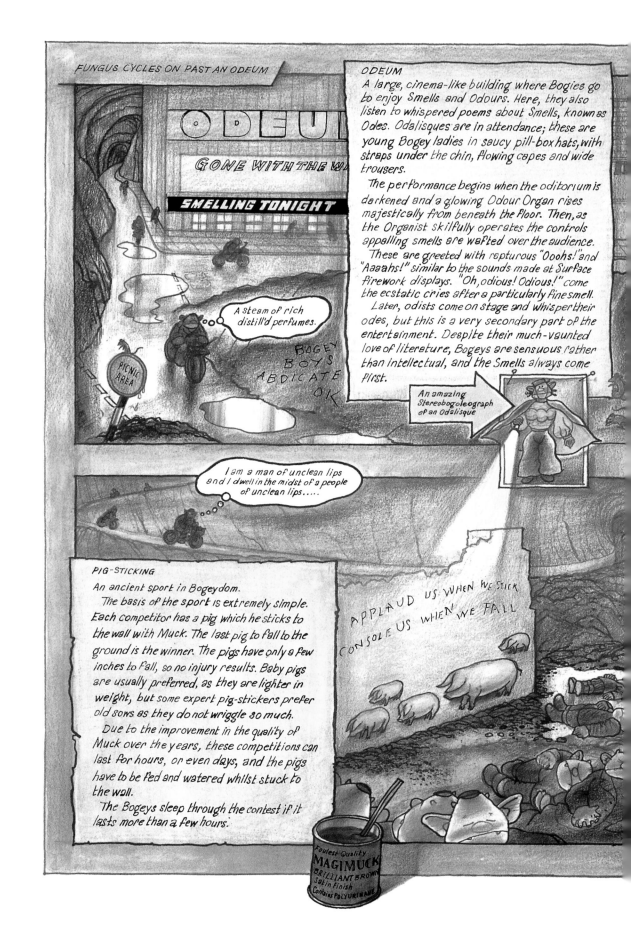

FUNGUS CYCLES ON PAST AN ODEUM

ODEUM

GONE WITH THE WI...

SMELLING TONIGHT

PICNIC AREA

A steam of rich distill'd perfumes.

BOGEY BOYS ABDICATE OK

ODEUM

A large, cinema-like building where Bogies go to enjoy Smells and Odours. Here, they also listen to whispered poems about Smells, known as Odes. Odalisques are in attendance; these are young Bogey ladies in saucy pill-box hats, with straps under the chin, flowing capes and wide trousers.

The performance begins when the oditorium is darkened and a glowing Odour Organ rises majestically from beneath the floor. Then, as the Organist skilfully operates the controls appalling smells are wafted over the audience. These are greeted with rapturous "Ooohs!" and "Aaaahs!" similar to the sounds made at Surface firework displays. "Oh, odious! Odious!" come the ecstatic cries after a particularly fine smell.

Later, odists come on stage and whisper their odes, but this is a very secondary part of the entertainment. Despite their much-vaunted love of literature, Bogeys are sensuous rather than intellectual, and the Smells always come first.

An amazing Stereobogoleograph of an Odalisque

I am a man of unclean lips and I dwell in the midst of a people of unclean lips.....

PIG-STICKING

An ancient sport in Bogeydom.

The basis of the sport is extremely simple. Each competitor has a pig which he sticks to the wall with Muck. The last pig to fall to the ground is the winner. The pigs have only a few inches to fall, so no injury results. Baby pigs are usually preferred, as they are lighter in weight, but some expert pig-stickers prefer old sows as they do not wriggle so much.

Due to the improvement in the quality of Muck over the years, these competitions can last for hours, or even days, and the pigs have to be fed and watered whilst stuck to the wall.

The Bogeys sleep through the contest if it lasts more than a few hours.

APPLAUD US WHEN WE STICK
CONSOLE US WHEN WE FALL

Foulest Quality
MAGIMUCK
BRILLIANT BROWN
Satin Finish
Contains Polyurethane

YE OLDE BOGEY BATTERYES

These ancient structures are found near the borders of Bogeydom, and were made for defence against Napoleybogey.

The walls of the batteries were built of soggy Muck to make them difficult for the enemy to climb. The Quaker Guns * at the top were calculated to inspire fear in the hearts of the enemy when viewed from a distance. (All Bogey guns are made of wood. They make no noise, have no ammunition, and do not fire. Long ago, Bogeys realised that metal guns did far more harm than good, so wooden ones were introduced. These have been found to be much more satisfactory, as they are silent and harmless.)

However, the wooden guns were so rotten, they fell to pieces when ever they were moved. The dummy wooden cannon balls were used by the gunners for playing bowels (Bogey bowls) though they were of little use even for this purpose, because they were _Bogey_ balls and therefore not round and consequently rolled about in a promiscuous fashion.

As the Bogeys had no idea from which direction Napoleybogey would come, the Quaker Guns were, of course, quaquaversal.

* QUAKER GUN: a wooden gun mounted to deceive the enemy.

POSTERS

Bogey posters do not advertise coming events; they advertise past events. By the time a Bogey sees the poster, the event which it announces has long since passed. Consequently, he does not need to write down times and dates, book tickets or travel, and can thus proceed with his normal indolent life in peace.

TIDDLYWINKS

Bogeymen are devoted to the game of Tiddlywinks, probably because it is silent and requires no exertion. As with most Bogey games, the object is to achieve a draw. This is not difficult, as Bogey tiddlywinks are made, not of bone, but of dried Muck. As a result, they usually snap in two when pressed one against the other and in damp weather they become soggy and useless.

The pot into which the tiddlywinks are aimed is filled with dirty water and if, by any chance a tiddlywink should fall into the pot, it instantly dissolves.

173

Unpublished *Fungus* sketches
Top: a Bogey umbrella
Above: a Bogey tramp

From this first notion sprang the Bogeyman – the figure that satisfyingly united the folkloric bugaboo that parents (though not his own) once conjured to frighten children with, and the 'bogey' that made them laugh because it meant a lump of snot. Fungus's world evolved as Briggs became more and more fascinated by the possibilities of the place where he lived. Briggs lost himself in the detail of a universe in which cold, wet, dirty and slow are desirable, and warm, dry, clean and fast – the characteristics of the world where we, the 'Drycleaners', live – are abhorrent.

He also spent nearly three months going through his dictionary page by page, looking for 'words that sounded Bogeyish or suggested Bogey ideas. I had used the same dictionary ever since I was a student in the fifties. Much later I realized it was published in 1918! Television is not mentioned in it.' He still has, he says, 'half a filing cabinet' of research that was never used – Bogey sports, religion, hobbies. Often there is a splendid serendipity about the meanings of the words he found: that 'barathrum', for instance, meant 'pit, chasm, or abyss of muck' – the perfect word for a Bogey bathroom, or that 'tyre' meant 'curdled cream or milk, beginning to sour'. It followed, of course, that this is what Bogey bicycle wheels are filled with.

There are literary games in the book as well as all the wordplay. The Bogey public library, or 'liberality', has shelves of identifiable novels whose titles have been changed to incorporate the word 'bogey', from Arnold Bennett's *The Grim Smile of the Five Bogeymen* to H. G. Wells's *Love and Mr Bogeyman*. Some take advantage of an existing similarity, as in *Tono Bogey* for Wells's *Tono Bungay*. In others the fun is in the anarchic improbability and the mad image a title conjures, as in *A Room with a Bogey*, for Forster's *A Room with a View*. Briggs points out that these books are in alphabetical order of author (at least as far as the first letter of the surname – Lee precedes Lawrence and Waugh follows some of the Wells). The literary-minded can compete with their friends to name all the originals.

One of the books on the liberality shelves was the subject of a surprising coincidence. In the 'hobbies and pastimes' section (such books as *Pulverulence and Derbyshire Neck* or *Grouts, Dregs and Lees*) is a book title Briggs made up called *Rotten to the Core: A Biography*. Eight years later a biography with this same title was published. It was written by Francis Selwyn and the subject was George Neville Heath, the murderer who was hanged in 1946. He happened to have gone to Briggs's school, Rutlish School in Merton, and while Briggs was at school the boys followed the case with fascination. 'In the lunch hour we used to rush out and buy the newspapers.' Neville Heath had only recently left, and when a text book was found with Heath's name in it, the boys auctioned it.

No-holds-barred grossness and erudite wordplay are the two salient features of Fungus's world: Bogeymen thrive on grottiness and think poetic thoughts: 'Bogeys frequently think in quotations – usually misquotations.' (Even the language of Bogey policemen is high-falutin': 'You've fill'd the air with barbarous dissonance,' says the officer attending a noisy disturbance.) It is an odd combination. Why create a character who is both squalid and cerebral? One source of inspiration is the slightly adapted Southey poem (originally about a pig) which forms the epilogue of the book and brings together the ideas of filth and philosophizing. It asserts, "tis a very honourable thing/To thrive by dirty ways,' and says, 'The Bogey [for Pig] is a philosopher, who knows/No prejudice.' The juxtaposition of these two characteristics caught Briggs's imagination. For someone whose mother was fastidious – a lady's maid who cared about keeping things clean and proper – and unintellectual, there seems to be in inventing such a character as Fungus a kind of teenage rebellion. The book was published after his mother's death, but, Briggs admits, she would have been puzzled and disturbed by it.

Certainly the book has always appealed to teenagers, and to students in particular. After all, squalor and intellect are both strands of the archetypal student experience: you discuss ideas into the night and no one cleans the loo.

The Oxford University magazine, *Isis*, was particularly delighted with Fungus when he appeared in 1977: 'A figure to tower above such cultural colossi as Albert Camus, T. S. Eliot and Johnny Rotten. One name and one alone will reek throughout the endless corridors of eternity – that of Fungus the Bogeyman.' The choice of comparable icons shows that Fungus was perceived as a figure who had something to say about alienation and disaffection. He was a suitable hero for an age of punk, when propriety or 'niceness' was the enemy.

Below: 'barbarous dissonance' in *Fungus the Bogeyman*

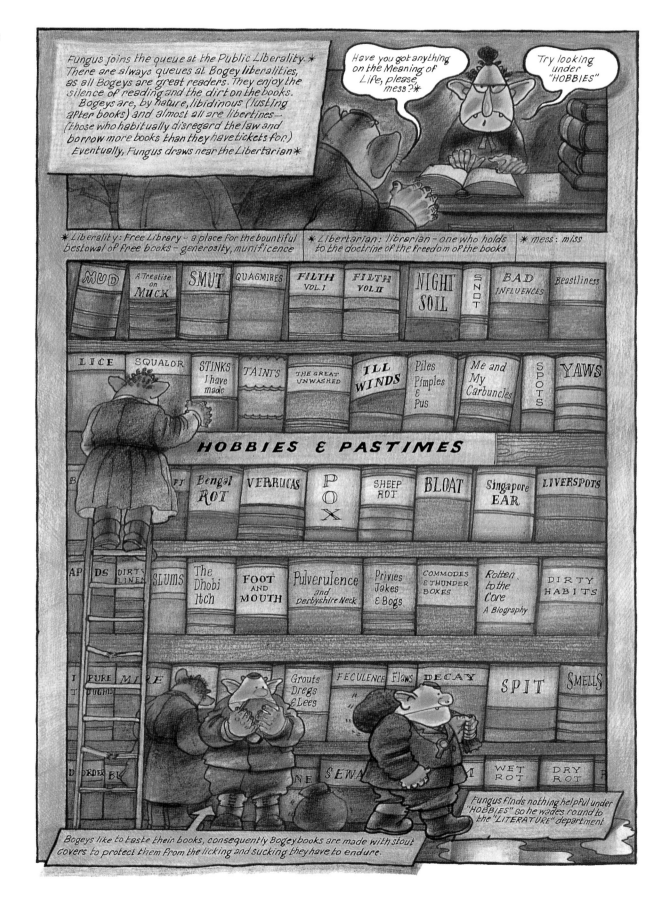

It must be pointed out, regrettably, that there is very little original Bogey literature.

Bogeys have very small tops to their heads; consequently, their brains are too small for the production of great literary works, such as this book you are reading.

Most Bogey books are taken from The Surface and are selected for their closeness to Bogey thought and feeling, or somewhat crudely adapted to fit Bogey themes.

This sad fact is never acknowledged by Bogeys. Over the years they seem to have successfully repressed all memory of it, and now genuinely believe their literature to have been entirely created by Bogeys.

(The pages of Bogey books are made of plastic to withstand the damp of the Bogey world. This is why they are so thick.)

THE GRIM SMILE OF THE FIVE BOGEYMEN · ANNA OF THE FIVE BOGEYS · BOGEYMAN STEPS · Summoned by BOGEYS · The BOGEY in WHITE · The MOON BOGEY · The Celestial Bogeyman · A Room with a Bogey · Under the Bogeywood Tree

Far From the Madding Bogey · The Return of the Bogey · A Portrait of the Artist as a Young Bogeyman · CIDER WITH BOGEY · Lady Chatterley's Bogey · The Plumed Bogey · BOGEY MY BOGEY · Love Among the Bogeymen · The Virgin and the Bogey

LITERATURE

The Bogeymen She Keeps · THE FLIGHT FROM THE BOGEYMAN · Nightmare Bogey · A la Recherche de Bogeys Perdus · THE MAN WHO WATCHED THE BOGEYMEN GO BY · Memoirs of a Bogeyhunting Man · Oh! What dross!* The richness of our literary heritage! · TONO BOGEY

The History of Mr Bogey · MR BOGEY SEES IT THROUGH · Put out More Bogeymen · VILE BOGEYMEN · BLACK BOGEYMEN · BOGEYMEN AT ARMS · OL...ND · Love and Mr Bogeyman

* dross: scum, refuse, rubbish, anything impure or good

Did you find what you wanted, *cheep?

No, but I got a storybook for my dumpling and a book of prose* for me.

Read a dull book and have a good sleep, that's what I always say

Yes, I suppose so, Boibye

FUNGUS LEAVES THE LIBERALITY AND CYCLES SLOWLY DUMPWARDS...

*cheep: dear. Bogish slang is often a simple reversal of the Surface word.

*prose: poetry (Bogeys always confuse the two)

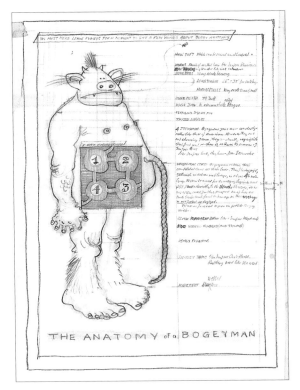

Above: a preparatory sketch for *Fungus the Bogeyman*
Below: the page as it appeared in the finished book

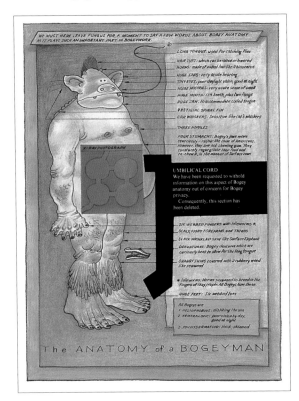

The critic Philip Hensher has described *Fungus the Bogeyman* as 'Dickensian' and 'baroque'. The elaborateness of the world it imagines, and of its associated language, was acknowledged to be one of its most impressive qualities.

The most hostile review was from the magazine *Reveillé*, which described Fungus as 'porn for the pre-potty trained', although the book is not actually coprophiliac. The Bogey public lavatory was censored in Briggs's original, as a joke. He didn't want to draw it. This was the first black patch. Other black patches appeared later, on the insistence of his publisher. In one case, two words are censored from a couplet of John Donne, which should have read: 'Rank sweaty froth thy mistress' brow defiles,/Like spermatic issue of ripe menstruous boils.' 'Spermatic' and 'menstruous' were felt to be too much (although the meaning of 'menstruous' is uncertain, and might merely have been a corruption of 'monstrous').

The other amendment insisted upon by the publisher was in the picture that showed that Bogeys still have their umbilical cords. This part of the anatomy was blacked out. As a metaphor for the fact that we all carry our connection with our mothers through life, though, this image has its touching interpretation. Again it implies that motherhood is an underlying (if perhaps unconscious) theme of the book. Certainly this is a book that is implicitly concerned with our

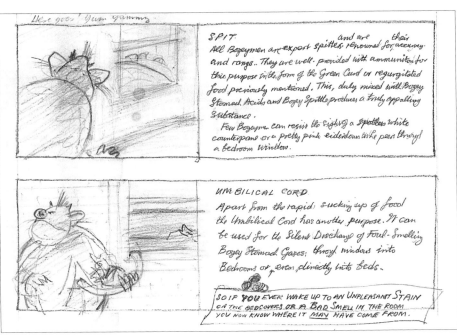

Preparatory sketches of the
umbilical cord in action

beginnings and our ends. It wallows in the pleasures of getting your hands dirty, like children making mud pies – and in fact Briggs got his own hands dirty, making the endpapers with handprints in green gouache, suggesting a Bogeyman's webbed fingers. All this smacks of nostalgia, harking back all the way to our primeval beginnings.

Although Briggs worked on this book intensively for two years, he had no real confidence that it would ever be published. 'I just had to do it,' he says. 'It became an obsession.' He doubted its future not so much because he thought it shocking, but because he feared it was 'too long-winded and tedious' to find general approval.

Julia MacRae at Hamish Hamilton immediately recognized the book as 'a work of glorious and provocative originality', but she also confesses that she was 'more than a little disconcerted', not least because the library market at the time was so important to children's publishers. After the success of *Father Christmas*, which, despite a touch of unconventional earthiness, was a huge hit as a children's book, *Fungus* was 'going to startle a lot more people than me'. She thought a little toning down would avert howls of protest from the more conservative book buyers in schools and libraries. With hindsight, she says, 'I think I was wrong. Twenty-five years later my reaction seems faintly ludicrous.' At the time, though, she was squeamish about Fungus's umbilical cord: 'I couldn't bear it.' Briggs reacted impishly by making the blacked-out patch much larger than the area taken up by the original.

The umbilical cord was originally used by Bogeys to poke in through windows and discharge noxious gases into bedrooms. MacRae had it replaced with a Bogey Stick. She also censored a joke in the text. Bogeys go to the cinema-like Odeum to enjoy smells (instead of movies) and a majestic Odour Organ rises from the floor, operated by the Organist. MacRae had the joke about onanism that appeared here removed.

The book was launched, appropriately, underground, with a party in the crypt-like Ludgate Cellars, where the walls tend to drip moisture. The food and drink were green, and the staff of the publishers wore T-shirts with Fungus hands crawling across the chest and the slogan FUNGUS FEELS FOR YOU.

Inscription in Julia MacRae's copy of *Fungus*

Raymond signing books at the *Fungus* launch party

Cover of *Fungus the Bogeyman Plop-Up Book*

Lookalike

Bogeyman   **Clarke**

The astonishing success of *Fungus* – which swiftly sold 325,000 copies – gave rise to the possibility of spin-offs, notably *The Fungus Plop-Up Book* (1982), which, unlike the original, did venture into a Bogey lavatory. Briggs's only contribution to Ron van der Meer's paper engineering for this was that he invented a way for Fungus's trousers to come down. In the end this was not used. Fungus's trousers were opened instead, which was, as Briggs says with satisfaction, much ruder.

The publishers came up with other plans, including *The Fungus the Bogeyman Book of Manners*, *Fungus the Bogeyboy: The Prequel*, and *A Bedtime Bogey Book: Stories to Give You Nightmares*. Terry Gilliam made a pilot film, with writing by Terry Jones, Neil Innes and others, using animatronics. In this, four people operate Fungus, a tiny actor in costume and full head mask, another actor speaks the words and two electronic technicians operate ear and lip movements. Mike Gruskoff, the Hollywood producer, worked on another film project for months and Richard Eyre tried to get a musical production together for the National Theatre. None of these projects was realized. However, at long last, in autumn 2003 a three-part BBC television series will be shown. Fungus has become a lasting icon. In 1999 Childline, the children's telephone helpline charity, raised £55,000 in one month selling £1 badges of Fungus and the Snowman at two chains of stores. In 2002, twenty-five years after the book was published, the satirical magazine *Private Eye* made a joke of the resemblance between Fungus and a politician (Charles Clarke, the new education secretary), safe in the knowledge that Fungus's was still a face that everyone could picture (in 2002 Clarke's was much the more obscure). Passionate fans remembered the book from their childhood, and passed it on to their equally passionate children. One woman even recorded on the internet the observation that she 'wanted to marry a man like Fungus – and did!' Fungus became a pin-up after all.

Another consequence of the book's success was that Briggs was asked in 1987 to write some 'monologues by Fungus' for radio, to be read by the actor Brian Blessed. He wrote them, but now cringes at the circumstances of the broadcast. It happened that on the day of the recording Myra Hindley was leading police to the graves of murdered children on the moors a short distance from the Manchester studio concerned. Unfortunately, the monologues included the idea of Fungus digging up disgusting things. It was, for that time and place, horrifically inappropriate. Suddenly a lack of squeamishness was not what was called for. Changes were made, but they felt to Briggs like a botched job. The monologues have never been made public as originally written, not least because they now had unhappy associations for the author.

Fungus the Bogeyman also became a 'plop opera' with music and lyrics by Mike Carter and Corin Buckeridge – despite the fact that Bogeys talk in whispers and hate music. The opera went along with Briggs's book up to a point, and then invented a twist in the plot in which young Mould rebels and falls in love with cleanliness, and even Fungus is revealed to be a secret collector of toilet rolls, which Mildew is horrified he might use. The umbilical cord came out of hiding, though: Mould appeared on stage naked with the cord trailing.

Briggs did think once that he would produce four sequels to Fungus, and did some early drawings, though these, like many of Briggs's fledgling ideas, never reached maturity, as he distracted himself with other projects. In the first sequel, Fungus, a peacemaker at heart, dreams of healing the breach between the Drycleaners and the Bogeys, and thinks, when he finds a Michelin Guide to Paris in a dustbin, that the upper and lower world might be brought together by setting up a tourist industry for Bogeydom. Being a Briggs aspiration, it all goes wrong. No tourists arrive.

The book was to be called *Fungus and the Michelin Man*. In it, Fungus writes to Monsieur Michelin, who is made out of tyres like the company's advertising symbol, and invites him to Bogeydom to produce a guide. Michelin accepts and is introduced to Bogey culture, art, restaurants and customs. Michelin becomes, like many readers, very attached to Fungus, and admires him. But he knows that his guide must tell the truth about Bogeydom, and that if it does, no one will come. He hates having to hurt Fungus.

Meanwhile Fungus, in his home-made Customs Officer's cap, sits in his Customs shed waiting for the flood of tourists to come pouring in . . .

Rough drawings for the unpublished
Fungus and the Michelin Man

must make a list of things I need.

Surface boots —— (Co-respondent shoes)

~~wide bottom~~ Surface trousers.

Long Surface overcoat

Scarf.

Wig.

False-beard & moustache

Hat.

dark-glasses for light

Chewing gum for ears.   Red make up

gloves

Brief case.

BOGEY BOOK SHOP

Rough drawings for the unpublished *Fungus* sequels. This page: Fungus disguised as a Drycleaner book salesman, in *Fungus and the Bumper Book of Bogey Verse* Opposite: Fungus fails to make Bogey beeves fly in *Fungus and Father Christmas*

The third *Fungus* book was to be *Fungus and the Bumper Book of Bogey Verse*. After the failure of Bogey tourism, Fungus realizes his approach was too sudden, and that he should begin more gently by introducing Drycleaners to Bogey culture. He decides to distribute a book of Bogey poetry (which is a hideous pastiche of Surface literature) and visits the Surface in disguise to arrange the publication of 56 million copies. He assumes that the Drycleaners will need one each.

Fungus and the Triumphs of Bogey Technology was to follow. Fungus has another idea. 'Trade! That is the answer. That is how civilization spread. Trade, then culture and literature, then tourism last of all.' This sequence would lead to friendliness, trust and even love. Too late, Fungus realizes that to trade with Drycleaners Bogeys will have to become more like them: efficient, fast, clean, noisy. Telephone bells will actually have to ring. The postal barges pulled along canals by somnolent beeves will have to speed up. Bogey life will be ruined. Fungus reveals his spiritual side and prays to the Great Boil above, 'Please let it be another failure. If I can only be a failure this time I can die happy.' 'As the only thing Bogeydom had to export was tons and tons of Muck and a certain amount of Slime, failure was guaranteed,' says Briggs. It is a rare Briggsian moment of things working out as hoped: but only because a character wants to fail.

Briggs also worked on *Fungus and Father Christmas*, which would have been a remarkable meeting of two of his own protagonists. In it Fungus meets Father Christmas on a rooftop and is amazed to hear what he does. He tries to persuade Santa to extend his round to Bogeydom. 'Not blooming likely!' is the response. 'I've got more than enough to do already. Do it yourself.' Fungus does. He decides to become the Bogey Father Christmas. He spends months building a 'sludge' out of rotten wood and training two Bogey beeves, called Slush and Turbid, to fly. 'At last he is ready to set off,' explains Briggs. 'Then he realizes he hasn't got any presents.'

Although Fungus failed to break into Surface book publishing, he did find his way into *The Penguin Dictionary of Modern Quotations* and also onto an album by Paul McCartney, *McCartney II* (1980). The track, 'Bogey Music', was part of the music for a film which was never completed.

The actor Bob Hoskins always wanted to play Fungus in a film, too, 'That's the story of my life, that is – I *am* Fungus!'

RAYMOND BRIGGS

11 Fungus inspects his trousers which have been marinading overnight. [*Fungus the Bogeyman*]

12 Bogeys are, by nature, libidinous (lusting after books) and almost all are libertines ~ (those who habitually disregard the law and borrow more books than they have tickets for). [*Ib.*]

From *The Penguin Dictionary of Modern Quotations*

Gentleman Jim (1980)

Jim Bloggs the lavatory cleaner also knows the bitter experience of things going wrong. He is thwarted in his plans both by his own lack of education and by red tape. Briggs says the book was inspired by a conversation with his partner's son Tom, who said: 'When I grow up I don't want to go to work.' He intended to live in a cave and build campfires and eat rabbits. Briggs found himself explaining how you can't light fires on other people's land, and spelling out the regulations that would make Tom's fantasy impossible – until the boy was practically in tears. It set Briggs thinking about what it would mean if an adult tried to put childish dreams into practice. How, if you wanted to be a cowboy, you couldn't just go and be one. You'd have to have a passport, visa, firearms certificate and export licence for a gun, work permit, insurance, money . . .

Jim has both the innocence of a boy and the malaise of a middle-aged man. He takes up again the existential angst of Fungus, as if carrying Fungus's vague mid-life crisis a step further and acting on it (Fungus only did so in the non-existent sequel) as he tries to find a way out of his unsatisfactory life. But Jim's ideas of an exciting life come principally from films and *Boy's Own* style fiction – he'd like to be a tail gunner or a highwayman. There is some incongruity in his notion of being an artist, since this is not generally the stuff of boys' adventure stories, but Briggs has taken the opportunity to make fun of attitudes to his own profession: 'Crumbs! You can't need much brains to be a <u>Artist</u>. You wouldn't think you'd need The Levels to be a <u>Artist</u>, would you?' The lack of educational qualifications or Levels – 'they give them these things at school nowadays' – is what Jim believes bars him from life's more glamorous possibilities: 'All we got [at school] was a Bible and a thick ear.' There is an irony in the fact that Briggs illustrates this fantasy of the glamour of the artist's life with scholarly references that, though appropriate for the theme, Jim himself would not recognize: the nudes that titillate Jim are careful copies of an Ingres Odalisque and a Correggio of Io seduced by Jupiter as a cloud. (Jim's fantasy of the Highwayman's swooning girlfriend, by contrast, is a portrait of the pretty young bookshop owner he buys his adventure stories from.)

In the end it is Authority that does for Jim. His mistakes, from parking a donkey on a yellow line to building a stable without planning permission, are the mistakes of a child ignorant of the regulations. He innocently tries to rob people on the highways, and his dreams put him in prison.

Briggs says his parents were terrified of doing anything wrong, and had a great respect for Authority. In *When the Wind Blows*, Jim and Hilda too trust that if only they follow idiotic regulations all will be well. Briggs says he has inherited this anxiety to some extent. 'I feel it about income tax forms. I'm always worried about getting that wrong.'

One of the joys of *Gentleman Jim* is the way the drawing conjures the grim facelessness of jobsworths and bureaucrats. Some of the Authorities that intimidate Jim are carefully characterized: snooty shopkeepers and red-faced park-keepers and RSPCA inspectors, for instance, but they all have narrow slits for eyes that don't look at you. The traffic warden is reduced to a featureless blank – with just a line for a nose and a Hitler moustache; the council surveyor is stylized to boxiness and angles; and the judge who sends Jim down is just a nose in a wig, until he reveals himself to be mad and a demented expression emerges.

The frames express too the isolation of the little man. Filmic sequences make him ever smaller in the landscape or lead him down

Jim has acquired a donkey he has christened Black Bess, and is attempting to fulfil his dream of becoming a highwayman

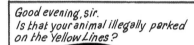

186

Who was that at the door, dear?

It was Someone in Authority. Another Official.

Oh my goodness!

They're after me before I've even started, Hilda. I expect it's due to modern security methods.

Oh dear!

What did he want, dear?

He's given me a Sums and he's going to commital me about the Pence or something, he said.

I must keep Black Bess in the back garden, dear. Because the yellow lines are illegal.

Oh, I see, dear

NEXT DAY Good afternoon! Mr. Bloggs? Inspector Parker – jolly old R.S.P.C.A. We understand you are keeping a donkey here?

Yes, that's right. I'm going to be a Highwayman.

We've been informed that the jolly old donkey is insufficiently housed and inadequately fed. What?

No sir, not really sir... it's that at this moment in time I'm insufficiently organised at present, sir. I didn't know they eat all day, sir...

So the jolly old donkey is out in all jolly weathers? What?

Well, er... yes. Hilda won't have it in the house because of the – you know....

Well, Mr. Bloggs, I suggest you build a shelter for this jolly old donkey at once and see that it is fed and watered regularly....

...otherwise the jolly old R.S.P.C.A. will have to take jolly old legal proceedings against you. Is that jolly clear, what?

Yes, sir. Thank you, sir.

Good day!

Crumbs! Jolly old proceedings!

one-way streets where big yellow arrows point the inexorable direction of his life. When he is picked up by the police, the car retreats into the distance so that Jim's ineffectual protestation, 'I wanted to give to the Poor' is dwarfed by the vastness of the empty motorway at night. Briggs effectively uses emptiness to express loneliness and helplessness. At the end of *The Snowman*, too, the discovery that the snowman has melted is shown in one final frame in the middle of a white page.

Gentleman Jim is another example of Briggs's talent for the poignancy of little lives. Jim's wife, whose face appears only intermittently, gets a touching, full-face moment when it is revealed that at heart she shares her husband's longing for romance and glamour. In his fantasy of going out west, he tells his wife she will be a saloon girl. When the practicalities cause Jim to abandon the cowboy plan, his wife's response is full of unexpected wistfulness: 'Oh, I see. So I won't have the blonde wig and the fishnet tights, then?'

Jim's wife quickly reconciles herself to disappointment. 'Perhaps it would not have been suitable,' she says. This is another characteristic of Briggs's little people, that they make the best of things, and put on a brave face. This is what Jim and Hilda – apparently the same individuals, later retired to the country – do when they reappear in *When the Wind Blows* and face the nuclear holocaust. It is their slightly idiotic cheerfulness that makes the ending of *Gentleman Jim* oddly happy. Jim's wife's loyalty mitigates his sentence, even if she is anxious not to miss her train after visiting time. Meanwhile Jim, who resigns himself to his punishment on the grounds that he 'got ideas above my station', finds pleasure in the possibility of getting some education inside, and in the fact that prison is the one place where a man with experience as a lavatory cleaner is an expert. In a way, prison offers him some of the opportunities he craved.

Unlucky Wally (1987)
Unlucky Wally Twenty Years On (1989)

If Wally swims in a lake, he usually finds the Frog Spawn. Afterwards, there is always Tapioca for tea.

EAT UP WALLACE, THERE'S A GOOD BOY

From *Unlucky Wally*

Unlucky Wally was one of Briggs's commercially less successful works. It had one problem in particular: that the cartoon style of illustration and Briggs's reputation as a children's author led people to assume it was a children's book, when it isn't. The character of Wally, for whom everything goes wrong, is not just about slapstick and silliness. It is also the story of Wally's sexual anxieties. There is a flashback to the *Fungus* theme of revoltingness: hairs in the soup, slugs in a sandwich, flatulence, but there is also Wally's worry about the unevenness of his testicles, and, in the sequel, his flirtation with pornography, his unconsummated visit to a prostitute, and his passing fret about homosexuality. And it becomes apparent that the book was not really intended for young children when it gets to the word 'propinquity'.

Briggs now calls Wally a 'self-indulgence'. It is, he admits, an unkind self-portrait – as is evident from the way Wally is drawn. When asked how autobiographical the character is, he says 'completely', although this cannot be true. Wally fails the medical for the army, for instance: Briggs served for two years. Critics accused Briggs of cruel mockery of his character for personal traits that should not be made fun of. 'But the character was me,' says Briggs. 'I was making fun of myself.' The first book targets youthful gaucheness; the sequel, twenty years on, the indignities of ageing.

One episode is certainly autobiographical and poignantly prefigures *Ethel and Ernest*. Wally's parents die within a year of each other. When Wally visits his dead mother in hospital, she lies on a trolley with a packet of Kleenex and a carton of Vim near her head.

Grief in Briggs's books is often shown by depicting figures from the back. This is true, for instance, of the graveside figures in *The Tin-Pot Foreign General and the Old Iron Woman*, and of the boy when the Snowman has melted. It is a device that dates from early Renaissance painters; Giotto uses it too, although Briggs claims that this is coincidence. He did not knowingly borrow the idea. It is just that 'backs are more expressive than faces distorted by emotion'. Wally, after his mother's funeral, is another who stands with his back to the reader.

One of the pleasures of the Wally books, although they are sad as well as funny, is that the pictures add more of the story to the text. The words on each page describe at least one of the ways in which Wally is unlucky and the pictures can show other ways as well. So that, for example, when Wally goes on holiday, the words tell us that his room will be overrun with spiders. The picture tells us that he'll also look out on a grey townscape although the hotel was called Sea View, and that his pillow will be dirty, the ashtray overflowing, and even his tooth glass chipped. Elsewhere buttons pop off, flies gather on his sandwiches, and dog turds wait in his path, even as the words concentrate on other misfortunes.

When Wally first appeared, he polarized the critics. For every opinion there was a counter-opinion. Those who liked him recognized that Wally is Everyman and there is a bit of him in all of us, and they enthused effusively. Those who disliked him called the books 'unfunny and infantile', 'a dreadful misconception', and 'entirely pointless'. Both camps were quoted on the paperback.

Wally is, like Fungus, a bit repellent. But, like many Briggs characters, he is also an innocent who inspires our sympathy for having a bad time and not being able to help it.

From *Unlucky Wally*

The Man *(1992)*

One of Briggs's less innocent characters is the Man, who turned up in 1992, naked, demanding and about six inches tall, in the bedroom of a boy called John. His origins are never accounted for, and he requires food, clothing, shelter and care for several days, during which his novelty wears thin. The epigraph to the book is a Chinese proverb: 'After three days, fish and visitors begin to stink.' Briggs was, he says, 'thinking about what happens in friendships. That you can love someone and yet want to brain them the next day.'

The Man has another provenance too. 'I saw the Man,' says Briggs, 'as one of the borderline people in our society, the very old, the mentally ill or handicapped, dependent on others for virtually everything, who have to get by through the love of someone if they are lucky enough or are dependent on the more successful members of society. They are forced to be parasitic. Dependence makes the Man truculent and he's fed up because he'll never have ordinary things like a torch or radio.' He also thought of the million carers in the country looking after somebody else, who are under such pressure, however fond and devoted they are. 'There's a terrific amount of illness and breakdown amongst carers.' Briggs's own experience of caring for another person was with his wife, the painter Jean Taprell Clark. She was schizophrenic and looking after her was 'a full-time occupation, really, so your whole life was devoted to dealing with it. You never knew what each day was going to bring.' Jean died of leukaemia in 1973.

He began the book, though, with his usual straightforward premise. 'I simply tried to imagine what would happen if you woke up one morning and found a small man on the bedside table, that was all . . . Because of his extremely small stature he can't live in the normal world – can't work or have a job, can't travel on public transport or do anything ordinary people do. He can't even turn on a tap or get the milk in. So he's forced to live a parasitical life hiding in other people's houses. I didn't want to create a cuddly character, more a primitive person who is a survivor and does his best to make

sure he survives.' Smallness does not make the Man sweet.

From the start, the Man is difficult. He wakes John by throwing cough sweets at him, and immediately gives orders. He complains about the food he is given, and takes issue with everything. He is reactionary and plebeian. John, by comparison, is a nice, liberal middle-class boy who reads books about art and eats wholemeal bread. His assumptions are tested, though, by the attitudes of his visitor, and this, along with the Man's demands, puts a strain on their relationship. The boy loses his temper on the fourth day. By the fifth the Man has disappeared.

During his two years of National Service, Briggs was struck by the fact that, although he thought himself 'ordinary', with his working-class background and his grammar school education, he was already 'the one in a hundred' who had been through tertiary education. The vast majority of the other soldiers were interested only in 'beer, sex and football'. Briggs felt himself to be different from his fellow soldiers, but he found friends among them. The Man is like a small version of one of these army colleagues (without the explicit interest in sex – although there is room for speculation about why he turns up naked after a quick getaway, with an unidentified 'she' eventually bringing his clothes).

It is the first day of the Man's visit. He and John are getting acquainted but already the Man's irascibility is becoming apparent

Hey! What about this?
Table tennis net!
I could pin it up either side in the cupboard.
Make you a hammock.
OK?

Yeah! That's good.
You're a brilliant boy.

I've got you a bit of carpet.

Is it red?

No. Grey-green.

I prefer red.

I'M OFF NOW, JOHN.
WON'T BE LONG.

OK. 'Bye, Mum.

Coast clear now.
How about this bath?

Oh … er … yes, OK.
Come and see.

No!
Not in your bath!
Far too dangerous. Lift me out.
You'll have to get me something -
a container.

Well … um … what, exactly?

Use your imagination, boy!
Look in the kitchen.

OK.

What about this?
It's heat proof.

Hmm ... not very dignified.
Too transparent.
Never mind. It'll do.
Get some hot water.
And some cold.
So's to make a nice mix.

More hot.
Whoa! Not too much.
More cold.
Steady!
That's OK.
Got any Bath Foam?
I like Avocado or Peach Blossom.

We've only got Woodland Pine.

Never mind.
It'll have to do till you go shopping.
Mix it in. Lovely!
Put a pile of books to make steps.
That's what I usually do.

Usually do?
Do you do this often?

Of course. All the time.
I haven't got a place of my own.
We have to move about ...
Have to keep on the move.
We can't live on our own, see?
Getting old now, I'd like to settle down ...
but it never works out ...

Oh?

three days ...

What?

that's about the limit.

What is?

Never mind, boy.
I'm just rambling.

What am I going to do if Mum comes in?

Bung the bowl in the Secrets Cupboard with me in it.
Any shampoo?

There's Mum's "Caresse" or Dad's
Medicated Anti-Dandruff.

Give me the "Caresse".
I've got very sensitive skin.
<u>You</u> can do my hair.
Not too rough mind.
Be nice and gentle.

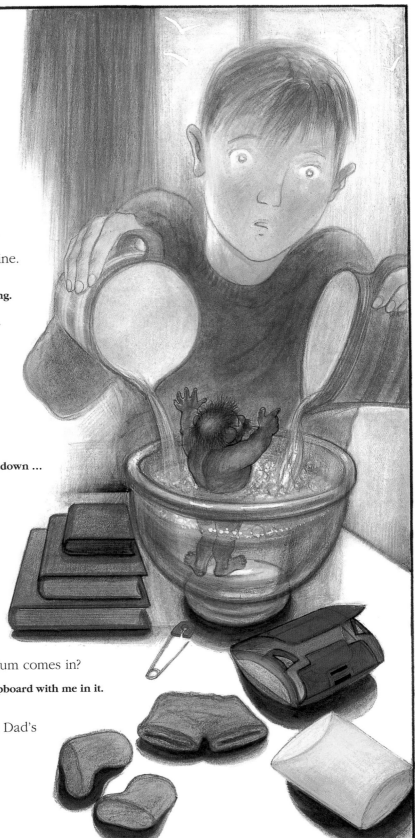

195

Got any chocolate?

No.
Mum's dead against sweets.

Nip out and get us some After Eights, will you?
They're nice and thin for my little mouth.

Um … I haven't got much money …
I don't suppose you -

"Naked came I into the world …"

I'll see what I can do.

Don't get any nutty muck.
The nuts hurt my little teeth.

Hey, Man! Man!
I've found some beer in the garage.
Left over from Christmas.
It's all dusty.

Good boy!
My goodness, it's Guinness, too!

And here's the After Eights.

Oh goody!
Yum! Yum!

I really like this place.
Your Mum being out a lot.
Very clean.
Nice and warm.
Good central heating system.
Oh, by the way, I've turned
the thermostat up a bit.
Your bedroom's a bit chilly.
Hope that's OK.

Oh yes … er … yes …
I should <u>think</u> so … um …
I don't suppose they'll notice.
I hope <u>Dad</u> doesn't …

**I watched the football this afternoon.
While you were out shopping.**

Oh?

Liverpool v Arsenal.

Oh.

Not interested?

No, not really.

What's your sport, then?

Don't like sport much.

**What!
None of it?**

Not really.

**Blimey!
What do you like then?**

Art.

**ART!
Gor Blimey!
What sort of art?**

Poetry and painting mostly.

**POETRY and PAINTING! PAH!
Can't <u>stand</u> soppy ART!**

Can't <u>stand</u> stupid SPORT!

I think I'll have a kip now.
Feel a bit knackered.
Do you mind keeping quiet for a bit?

No, no, not at all.
You go ahead.

Leave me the door open for some air.

Yes, of course.
I'll … er … go downstairs.
Got to go shopping anyway.

I'll have a cup of tea later.

Yes … yes … OK.

Got the list?

Yes.

Don't forget the Frank Cooper's Oxford.

No, OK.

Just a minute

Yes?

Before you go shopping -
Come here, boy. Pick me up.
Now listen. This is serious.

OK. I'm listening.

You've got to swear - not to tell <u>anyone</u> about me.

OK. I swear.

No one at all.
Not your mother. Not your father.
Not your friends.
No one.
TOP SECRET!

OK.

Remember - a secret is not a secret if more than two people know it.

Right.

No word to the Authorities -

Authorities?

Yes.
School, Town Council, DHSS, Police - that mob.
Nor the busybodies -

Busybodies?

Yes. Prodnoses, nosy parkers, tripe merchants -
mucky newspapers, tatty magazines, soppy book
publishers, twerp television, jabbering local radio -
manufacturers and distributors of tripe by the ton.
Tell <u>them</u> I'm here and they'll never let you alone.
Or me. You'll be famous for a day and I'll be
a comic turn. Our lives will be ruined.

So <u>swear</u>!

I swear.

Here -

Ouch!

Blood brothers!
United in blood
and secrecy!

The boy and the Man feel both affection for and hostility towards each other. What gives the book its substance is their debate, a debate between classes, between the educated and the uneducated, between the privileged and the disadvantaged, the able-bodied and the handicapped, the young and the ageing. Briggs's own relationship with his father lurks in this conversation – the boy, as one critic put it, 'on the way up, and the Man on the way down'. Or, as he has admitted, it is an exchange between different aspects of himself. It is, though, a meeting of equals. Neither character necessarily wins.

The text of *The Man* is all dialogue, with three different typefaces: John's speech in a regular font, the Man's utterances strident in bold, and John's parents calling in capitals from off-stage. The ensuing conversation encompasses religion, patriotism and the arts, all without being in the least turgid or dogmatic. It considers society's attitudes to outsiders and oddballs, and deliberately raises more questions than it answers, 'sending out ripples like a stone thrown into water', as Roger Woddis of the *New Statesman* put it. It turned out to be a book that inspired a lot of classroom discussions.

One aspect of the book that caused controversy was the Man's remarks about foreigners. He uses the word 'wogs' – but in a context in which he could be attributing the racism implicit in the word to the boy. 'This is a private kingdom, is it?' he says of John's home. 'The wogs begin at the front door?' One head teacher returned his signed copy to the publishers on the grounds that the use of this word made the book unsuitable for his school. The Man says that he 'hates foreigners', but at the same time he reveals that, for all the boy's political correctness, it may be that the youngster is the one with the most prejudices. He has good intentions, but makes demeaning assumptions about the Man because of his size, is patronizing and controlling, and has expectations of normality based on his own family as the standard.

Political correctness caused a significant change to the text. The Man originally launched into a tirade about foreigners (or about attitudes to foreigners) in which he listed every term of racial and national abuse he could think of – 'Pakis, chinks, frogs, fuzzywuzzies, eyeties, krauts, wops, wogs, paddies, sambos, jewboys, polacks, nignogs, gringos'. 'Wogs' was only one of the words in this list.

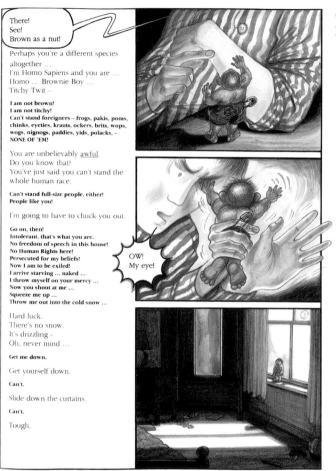

There!
See!
Brown as a nut!

Perhaps you're a different species
altogether ...
I'm Homo Sapiens and you are ...
Homo ... Brownie Boy ...
Titchy Twit –

I am not brown!
I am not titchy!
Can't stand foreigners – frogs, pakis, poms,
chinks, eyeties, krauts, ockers, brits, wops,
wogs, nignogs, paddies, yids, polacks, –
NONE OF 'EM!

You are unbelievably <u>awful</u>.
Do you know that?
You've just said you can't stand the
whole human race.

Can't stand full-size people, either!
People like you!

I'm going to have to chuck you out.

Go on, then!
Intolerant, that's what you are.
No freedom of speech in this house!
No Human Rights here!
Persecuted for my beliefs!
Now I am to be exiled!
I arrive starving ... naked ...
I throw myself on your mercy ...
Now you shout at me ...
Squeeze me up ...
Throw me out into the cold snow ...

Hard luck.
There's no snow.
It's drizzling -
Oh, never mind ...

Get me down.

Get yourself down.

Can't.

Slide down the curtains.

Can't.

Tough.

OW!
My eye!

Original page proof,
later revised

Julia MacRae was urged to remove some of the less current terms and revised it to: 'frogs, pakis, poms, chinks, eyeties, krauts, ockers, brits, wops, nignogs, paddies, yids, polacks'. But even this version was not thought to be acceptable. It was felt that publication alone would encourage the use of the terms. Briggs agreed to remove most of them. Arguably, the effect was then more pernicious.

Briggs believes that it is sometimes right to legislate about propriety in language. As a child and a young man he hated the now unacceptable word 'cripple', especially when his mother was faced with having to be in a wheelchair. He approves of elbowing such words out. But the idea behind the catalogue of xenophobic insults was to neutralize the terms by accumulating them, and also to demonstrate that everyone can be a target. The abuse was general, rather than particular, which defused it. Using one pejorative term seems more deliberate than using a host of them. Ironically, the book contains its own argument against this kind of censorship. The boy's response to the word 'wogs' is: 'Don't use words like that here. Mum would kill you.' The Man responds, 'She sounds like a nice, tolerant liberal sort.' Julia MacRae now thinks she should have held out against this change.

One other editorial change was the deletion of full-frontal nudity in this book. In the original dummy, the Man is flagrantly naked when he first appears. The drawing was altered for publication so that he is covering himself up, contorted into a more discreet pose.

Preparatory drawing for *The Man*, later modestly changed

Briggs spent two months writing *The Man*, another five laying out the design, and two years completing it in colour. It has more than 150 pictures, and a good deal of text. It is twice the length of most picture books. 'I got terribly depressed doing it – it was so repetitive. Each character appears over a hundred times. And those infernal trainers! Every time I drew them I had to make sure the number of lace holes was the same.' He drew from memory, so the settings are ones he knows – the house is the yellow-brick terrace with green sash windows that he grew up in. He drew his father's chair and his own bedside table. The boy also uses a mug with the Snowman on it. Again, Briggs combines fantasy with realism to ground his magic in ordinariness.

Difference is one of the themes of this book. Another is fame. The boy considers whether to make the Man's existence known. In the film script of *The Man* that Briggs later wrote, he gives three children a position in a debate about the fate of the Man: one argues that he should be allowed his privacy and freedom; another makes the case for scientific study and protection; and a third sees his appearance as an opportunity for profit and celebrity. *The Man* appeared as an audiotape with Michael Palin playing a gruff Man and William Puttock as the boy. The Man's position is that he wants no one to interfere with his life, particularly not the Busybodies: 'Prodnoses, nosy parkers, tripe merchants – mucky newspapers, tatty magazines, soppy book publishers, twerp television, jabbering local radio – manufacturers and distributors of tripe by the ton. Tell <u>them</u> I'm here and they'll never let you alone . . . Our lives will be ruined.' This is written with feeling, and it is hard not to hear in it some of the reasons for Briggs's legendary reluctance to court fame.

There was another objection to *The Man*. One correspondent complained about the scene in which the Man makes a pact with the boy by pricking fingers and mingling blood – a common playground practice in Briggs's youth, but unwise in an age of Aids. Anyone who writes for children encounters this problem: that there are those who perceive children's books as behaviour manuals which must set no bad examples. Briggs credits children with the sense to know what not to emulate.

Notwithstanding his height, the Man is an ordinary chap. But he also has symbolic aspects. He arrives quoting the Bible (his only reading matter, apart from the racing news), naked and hungry, like a biblical figure come to test the boy's charity.

One of his biblical quotations, Job 38:29, 'Whence came the Ice? Whose Womb hath gendered It?' suggests that he himself is a force of nature. He is nameless, like the gulls outside the window. He's earthy, hairy and rat-like ('He has to be to survive,' says Briggs). Although he is adamant that he is human and not animal, he also seems to represent the natural and the instinctive, being a creature of basic (if fussy) needs.

The Man is a test of patience, a creature of instinct and a force of nature. In other words he is like a child. As the boy is the Man's carer, the roles of adult and child are reversed. 'The boy becomes a parent who gets no thanks but – like a mother who grumbles endlessly but suffers when the children leave home – he likes doing it,' says Briggs. 'The Man is childlike and petulant, illiterate too, because he couldn't go to school.' Some have pointed out that the big safety pin that holds the Man's clothes together is like a nappy pin. A connection has been seen between the red-haired, demanding Man and the red-haired, demanding baby in *The Elephant and the Bad Baby*. One critic even found, in the final image, that the Man's discarded clothes – the bootees, safety pin and little knickers – were 'unmistakably the accoutrements of a dead baby', and that the boy's grief was equated with parental loss.

Like the stroppiest of us, the Man has moments of vulnerability. He wants to be cuddled in the night. He needs to be comforted like a baby when he is frightened. And he is sensitive. His lack of education is painful to him: 'There's nothing worse than being uneducated. You miss so much in life. It's like being only half alive,' he says, drawn wincing and cowed by the grief of it. We know that he feels deeply, too, because we see him from the back – that trademark Briggs understatement – as he contemplates the moon from the rooftops.

He worked his way too into the affections of the jury of the prestigious Kurt Maschler Award for an illustrated children's book. *The Man* won the 1992 prize, and Quentin Blake, chair of the judges, praised its 'extraordinary power of discovering myths, myths that we didn't know were there'. His fellow judge, Chris Powling, wrote, 'What Raymond Briggs does so well is invent mythical figures which remind us sharply of ourselves.' *The Man* also earned Raymond Briggs the accolade of Children's Author of the Year at the 1992 British Book Awards.

Ug: Boy Genius of the Stone Age (2001)

The Man's theme of a conversation between the middle-class, educated and artistically minded and the philistine working-class, born out of Briggs's own experience of intellectual distance from his parents, reappears in *Ug: Boy Genius of the Stone Age*, his witty and playful tale of a boy who has ideas ahead of his time and beyond the narrowness of his upbringing. 'It's the same in all my books. You have the intelligent younger generation questioning the assumptions of a less intelligent, less well-educated older generation.' It is satisfying for his young readers that the kids are the smarter ones.

Ug's ideas include using fire for heat and cooking, and inventing enclosures, irrigation and the wheel (though he can't think what it's for), and he almost manages to come up with wooden boats and the soft trousers he longs for. His father thinks his son should count himself lucky to wear trousers of hand-carved sandstone when his own generation had to put up with gritty granite. No one takes Ug up on any of his brainwaves, because this is a satire about the gap between the free-thinking intellectual and the small-minded conservative. Since all children think their parents are small-minded conservatives, the book is also an extended joke about the generation gap, in which both the older and the younger generation happen to be prehistoric. It's about the curiosity of the child opposed to the rigid thinking of the adult. The Briggsian pathos of the story comes from recognizing in Ug's parents any modern parents who don't appreciate their child's potential, from watching a small boy trying hopelessly to make himself heard, and from the hindsight by which we know that his family has missed out on some of the major milestones of civilization by not paying attention to their son. That the book ends with Ug's own adulthood, which reveals that all his imagination got him nowhere, is also typical – it reminds us of the unfulfilledness of Fungus and Jim.

Ug's mother rages: 'You kids today are never satisfied,' when Ug suggests building a house instead of living in a cave. Ug's father blames 'youth culture' when Ug uses sissily upbeat words like 'terrific'. Ug can't get through to either of his parents. Although his

Ug very nearly invents the wheel and the word for it

204

father has a glimmering of sympathy, his mother can't begin to understand Ug's desire for warmth, softness and niceness, or his aesthetic sensibilities. When he brings her flowers, she eats them. 'Mark my words – he'll go mad, that boy,' she says. 'He'll end up painting animals on the walls.' He does.

Julia MacRae took issue with Briggs about the last page. She thought it was a mistake to leap through the years until Ug is grown up and his parents are dead. She worried that this was confusing, as well as downbeat. Briggs chose not to take her advice, and left in the coda, which arguably gives the book more depth, as well as a punch line. It leaves the reader with a poignant sense of what might have been (although of course Ug could never have been a success; if his ideas had caught on, the Stone Age would have ceased to be the Stone Age). The book ends with an image that suggests what it means to grow up disappointed in the aspirations of your youth. There is also an autobiographical note in this last scene: the hero is an artist, who has outlived parents who once thought being an artist was a barmy idea.

Although this is a story about parents and children, with a theme that has to do with Briggs's own childhood experience, it is remarkable that, in his first solo picture book after *Ethel and Ernest*, Briggs's parents are, for once, absent from the drawing. One or both appeared in *Father Christmas*, *The Snowman*, *Fungus* (obliquely) and *Wally*. The house they lived in appeared in both *The Man* and *Father Christmas*. Ug's parents, Dug and Dugs, look nothing like Ethel and Ernest. It is as if with their joint biography he had finally drawn them and their home out of his system.

The Stone Age setting was triggered, says Briggs, by a question from his partner's son thirty years earlier: 'Why do they have trees?' Ug too wonders what the trees are for. Other than that, Briggs says, the book was born of the fact that 'I hate drawing modern objects – cars, buses, phones, etc., so a world with nothing but mud, bushes and stones was much easier to do.' There have also been unfounded suspicions about another source of the world of Ug in which even blankets and tennis balls are made of stone. 'Nobody believes I haven't seen *The Flintstones*,' says Briggs. 'I wish I had. I could have cribbed some ideas.'

The final page of *Ug*

*Ug tests his parents'
patience with his
persistent questions and
new ideas*

206

Anachronisms, explained by humorous footnotes, are a rich source of jokes in this book: 'The Ice Age will be here before you are!' shouts Ug's mother, trying to rouse her family. The book has no historical accuracy whatsoever, of course. That isn't the point. The fun, especially for older readers, is in the inaccuracy.

Briggs was also thinking about how it seems to take mankind an astonishingly long time to come up with its good ideas. Whole ages pass before new developments evolve. And even in modern times, he says, it surprises him how long, for instance, both sheets and elastic had existed before anyone thought of fitted sheets. 'In my childhood we wasted all that time tucking in. And the centuries it took to think of chimneys! Centuries more before it was realized the flues should be narrow, not wide, to draw the smoke away.'

He was interested, too, in the way inventions depend on each other. Ug gets as far as cutting out animal skins to make soft trousers, but since no one has yet come up with a needle and thread, progress is halted there. 'One genius doesn't necessarily come up with an idea, but many people build on previous ideas.'

Although Ug was received with delight by readers and critics alike, a murmur of protest (to which Briggs is no stranger) came from one quarter. This time the portrayal of Ug's mother as the impediment to his potential, as well as a shrieking and narrow-minded harridan, led to accusations of misogyny. One critic disliked the fact that Ug's mother is called 'Dugs' – an 'archaic and mildly obscene name'. Dug has the merit of sounding like a real man's name. Dugs was a whimsical next step in the sequence, with its apt double-meaning, though Briggs calls it rather a feeble joke. 'Perhaps I went a bit over the top with the mother,' he concedes, but children have responded with recognition to what the critic called her 'nagging harangue'.

Ug won the Silver Medal in the Smarties Award of 2001, voted for by children.

The Social Issues

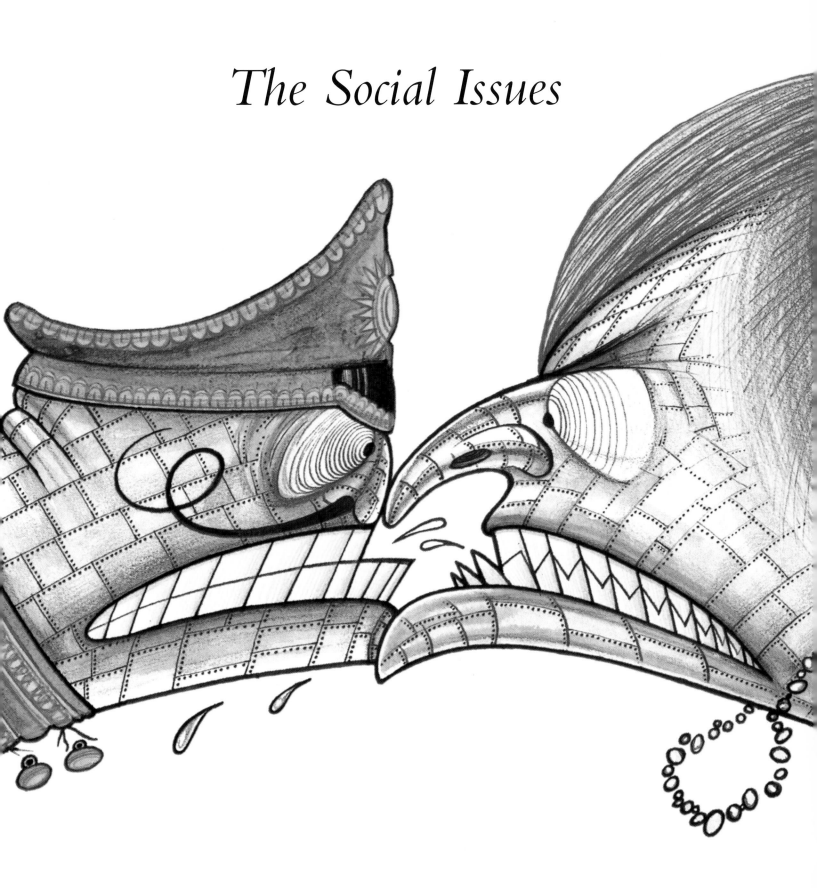

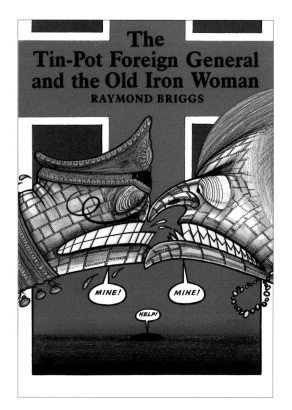

When the Wind Blows (1982)

IN 1980 *GENTLEMAN JIM* MARKED a change of direction in Briggs's work. With it he became a satirist. In that book the target was bureaucracy in general. In *When the Wind Blows* it is, more specifically and terrifyingly, the inadequacy of government preparations for a nuclear attack. The audience for this book, as well as for *The Tin-Pot Foreign General and the Old Iron Woman*, about the Falklands War, and for his biography of his parents, *Ethel and Ernest*, was now unequivocally adult. The empathy for the common man that was evident in *Father Christmas* had evolved into a political stand. These books changed our perceptions of real events. They showed us the human experience that slogans can bypass.

When Raymond Briggs was five, at the beginning of the Second World War, he was evacuated to stay with a couple of elderly aunts in Dorset. The aunts always kept three suitcases ready-packed in case of invasion by the Germans, so as to flee westwards as refugees. One night, recalls Briggs, 'amid the drone of bombers overhead, there came a sudden roar of engines and a deafening burst of machine-gun fire. It sounded very close. Aunt Betty shrieked, "Get the cases, Flo!" We hurried downstairs, pulled on coats over our pyjamas and nightdresses, seized the suitcases and stood there trembling. Quite where we were going, on foot, in the middle of the winter night, was not clear. In the end we went nowhere and returned to bed, unharmed but very frightened.'

In *When the Wind Blows*, Briggs imagines the unimaginable – a nuclear explosion – and creates characters who react like Aunt Flo and Aunt Betty. They do what they can in the face of a threat they do not understand, and their efforts are misguided and ridiculous but touching. Flo and Betty, on the suitcase occasion, overestimated the danger, while Jim and Hilda in *When the Wind Blows* underestimate it. Yet both cases demonstrate how horrors on a huge scale have an impact on individual lives, and can only be measured in the terms of those lives. Briggs also shows that tragedy can happen even to those who cannot comprehend it. Jim and Hilda, who are ignorant about radiation, and do not grasp the danger they are in, nevertheless come to a painful end.

Jim and Hilda Bloggs are drawn as the protagonists from *Gentleman Jim*, published two years earlier, in which a lavatory cleaner's aspirations for a more exciting life are thwarted by red tape. Once again the couple are victims of officialdom and authority: they follow the preposterous government guidelines for what to do in the event of a nuclear strike, and those guidelines are criminally inadequate. All the official instructions in *When the Wind Blows* came from real government documents, which eye-opening and distressing fact gives the book its political bite. Briggs, horrified by a television documentary about civil preparation for a nuclear attack, tracked down all the available literature, notably a leaflet called 'Protect and Survive'. Jim and Hilda's ludicrous preparations are those we were all being instructed to undertake.

Jim and Hilda look as they did in the earlier book, but in some ways their characters have changed. Jim, last seen in prison for flouting petty regulations he was too ill-educated to understand, is a more fluent reader than he used to be. In *Gentleman Jim* he expected that one of the benefits of prison would be the chance to get some education. If *When the Wind Blows* is really a sequel, he did get some. Now retired to a remote country cottage, Jim can at least read government documents, even if he is still too innocent to appreciate their pointlessness. But he hasn't changed enough to get difficult words right: he says 'innumerate' for 'innumerable' and 'commuters' for 'computers', for instance. He believes the Big Bang Theory has something to do with what happens when a bomb is dropped and that the Survival of the Fittest is about taking exercise. And he is confused by acronyms. He thinks the KGB is called the B. J. Key.

Hilda's ignorance is even greater. In some ways it protects her. Jim has some sense – though not a realistic one – of the danger of a nuclear bomb. Hilda has none. Neither of the two expects to die, but Hilda does not even expect things to change much. At the three-minute warning, she decides to take the washing in. After the bomb she puts her hair in curlers. She believes services will be restored, and visitors will come round. Like Jim, she does not grieve for their son Ron and daughter-in-law Beryl. It does not occur to either of them that they will be dead.

Ethel & Ernest
A True Story
RAYMOND BRIGGS

Opening pages: Jim Bloggs comes home from the Public Library

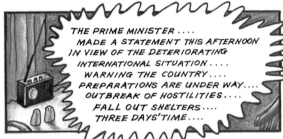

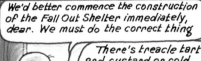

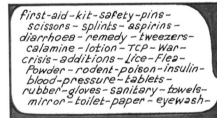

Jim and Hilda discuss the political situation

They say it's the correct thing to wear white. People in Hiroshima with patterned clothes got burned where the pattern was, and not so much on the white bits — even the buttons showed up

Yes, but they were Japanese

!!?

Is there a clean white shirt, dear? Ready for The Bomb?

You're not going to wear that nice new one I gave you for Christmas! I don't want that spoiled

You can wear your old clothes for The Bomb and save your best for afterwards

All right, dear. But is there an old white one? Without stripes. I don't want stripes all over me

Never heard such nonsense. We didn't think what colour clothes we had on in The War. Lucky to have any clothes at all with everything on coupons, and besides—

WE ARE INTERRUPTING THIS PROGRAMME

FOR AN OFFICIAL GOVERNMENT ANNOUNCEMENT

AN ENEMY MISSILE ATTACK HAS BEEN LAUNCHED AGAINST THIS COUNTRY

IN JUST OVER THREE MINUTES

God Almighty, ducks! There's only three minutes to go!!

Oh dear, I'll just get the washing in

COME BACK YOU STUPID FOOL AND GET IN THE SHELTER!

TAKE COVER

How dare you talk to me like that, James!

SHUT UP AND GET IN!

There's no need to forget our manners just because there's a war on

DO NOT LEAVE YOUR HOMES

SHUT UP I'M TRYING TO LISTEN!

STAY INDOORS

I've never heard such language in all my life

DO NOT LEAVE YOUR HOMES

FOR GOD'S SAKE SHUT UP!

LIE DOWN

Oh dear! I've left the oven on

GET IN! GET IN! GET IN!

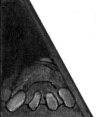

ON NO ACCOUNT TRY TO

The cake will be burned

The book is emotionally almost overwhelming, for many reasons. One is the magnitude of its subject – that it portrays our worst fear. The two white pages that convey the nuclear blast, with just an edge of pink, suggesting glow or burn, must be the scariest blank pages in literature. Another source of emotional power is the irony of the misapprehensions of Jim and Hilda: the fact that we know that things are so much more terrible than they appreciate. This irony is made explicit in the early part of the book by dark full-page drawings of armaments in readiness that lurk between the strip illustrations, with their sinister depiction of the build-up to nuclear war. After the explosion the irony depends on our understanding of the implications of radiation, which Jim and Hilda lack. For all this we recognize that, even with our superior knowledge, our efforts would be just as puny and ineffectual in the face of such horrors as theirs are.

Meanwhile comedy and tragedy are extraordinarily intertwined. It is laughable that Hilda is so preoccupied with trivia, and that Jim is so confused about world affairs, and at the same time such innocence is excruciatingly sad, and we are moved by the tenderness between the man and his wife. Even the last, agonizing pictures, in which Jim and Hilda make a ham-fisted attempt at prayer, and can't quite remember what words to use, manage to be both funny and terrible, and to draw together the book's themes of love, expressed in Jim and Hilda's endearments, and of innocent trust in authority – they pray because they think it might be 'the correct thing'. Daringly, Briggs makes gentle fun of Jim in the very last frame. He is moving into the valley of death, which makes him think of 'The Charge of the Light Brigade'. But the last words of the poem that he remembers are quite beside the point.

As became even more apparent when *Ethel and Ernest* was published, Jim and Hilda share characteristics with Briggs's parents. Hilda has something of Ethel's face and figure, and of her conservatism, fastidiousness and aspirations. She was the sort who wouldn't want her best cushions spoilt. But Jim and Hilda are 'dimmer', says Briggs, than his parents were. Ethel and Ernest were not well educated, but they were not so stupid as to have followed the government guidelines with such blind trust.

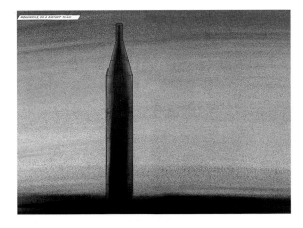

Armaments build up in *When the Wind Blows*

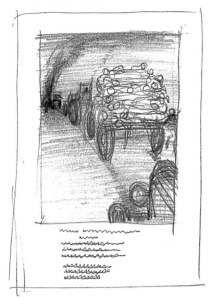

The boughs do shake and the bells do ring,
So merrily comes our harvest in,
Our harvest in, our harvest in,
So merrily comes our harvest in.
We're ploughed, we're sowed,
We're reaped. we're mowed,
We've got our harvest in.

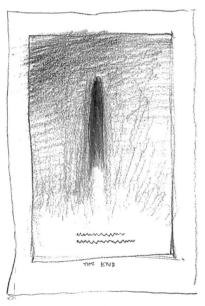

Here comes a candle to light you to bed,
Here comes a chopper to chop off your head

Two sketches for *How Many Days
Has My Baby to Play?*

Briggs's first suggested title for *When the Wind Blows* was *Mr and Mrs Bloggs and the Big Bang*. It was not popular in the US, where bang means the same as it does in the phrase 'gang bang' in British English. He is now much happier with the title he took from a nursery rhyme: 'Rock-a-bye-baby . . .' He liked the idea of suggesting something childlike, but was also struck, when he worked on illustrating nursery rhymes, with how much the rhymes were concerned with life and death, sex, money and greed. He once put together a whole book of nursery rhymes illustrated as if they applied to a nuclear confrontation. It was to be called *How Many Days Has My Baby to Play?* 'Merrily comes our harvest in', for instance, was accompanied by a drawing of a pile of bodies on a cart. 'It was astonishing how many fitted, once you had this idea,' says Briggs, citing other instances: 'If I die before I wake,/I pray the Lord my soul to take.' Not surprisingly, though, this gruesome anthology was never published.

When Julia MacRae received the manuscript of *When the Wind Blows*, she knew that this 'profound statement' would cause a stir, but she made, as she remembers it, no editorial alterations. In fact the publishers courted reactions: copies were sent to every Member of Parliament. Some responded. Left-winger Michael Foot acknowledged that it was 'topical'. Liberal leader David Steel (from the safety of the opposition benches) called it 'unnerving'. In the House of Lords, the Labour Peer Lord Elwyn-Jones came closest to confronting its message by saying that 'it raised the gravest questions of our time'. From the Prime Minister, Margaret Thatcher, there was silence. (She would find herself depicted in Briggs's work later.) The book was immediately a bestseller, however, and went on to sell more than 500,000 copies. It was translated into ten languages. Julia MacRae believes it 'changed the thinking of a generation of readers'.

The book was swiftly translated into other media. It became an animated film with the voices of Jim and Hilda spoken by John Mills and Peggy Ashcroft. Peter Sallis and Brenda Bruce took the roles in Briggs's own radio adaptation, which won the Broadcasting Press Guild award for the best radio programme of 1983. And then it became a West End play with Ken Jones and Patricia Routledge, opening in April 1983 at the Whitehall Theatre, not far from the Houses of Parliament.

Briggs and MacRae attended the first night together. They passed a demonstration on the pavement outside. Briggs recalls: 'A group of demonstrators from a movement led by Lady Olga Maitland, objecting to the anti-nuclear theme of the play, had taken rooms directly opposite the theatre. Red, white and blue bunting and Union Jacks hung from the windows, together with loudspeakers playing "Land of Hope and Glory". The music and speeches could be heard inside the theatre and as a result an air of tension hung over the whole performance.'

Briggs, not by nature an agitator, was not a member of the Campaign for Nuclear Disarmament until later. But he remembers what it was like to live through the real possibility of a nuclear attack, during the Cuban Missile Crisis in October 1962, which has been called the most dangerous month in human history. After US intelligence had revealed that the Russians were installing nuclear missiles in Cuba that were aimed at America, there was a stand-off that could have resulted in a nuclear conflict, started by either side. President Kennedy, trying to avert this, imposed a naval blockade of Cuba to stop Soviet ships bringing in arms. 'I remember the ship approaching the island, that Kennedy insisted must turn back. I remember feeling actual physical fear at the time. We were all wondering whether we would still be alive next week,' says Briggs. He recalls his relief when the ship turned round. (The crisis passed when Soviet President Khrushchev eventually gave in to US pressure to remove the missiles from Cuba.)

Written while there was still such a thing as the Cold War, *When the Wind Blows* was published at a time when the global nuclear threat to the West was perceived to be from Communism. But as long as there are nuclear weapons in the world, the book will always retain its power.

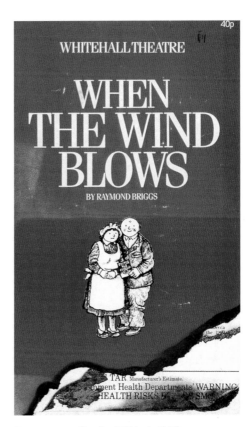

Programme for the Whitehall Theatre production of *When the Wind Blows*

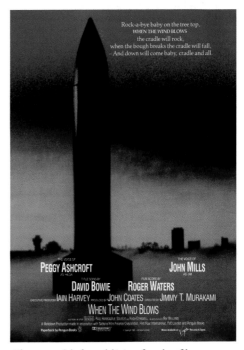

Above and left: publicity for the film

The Tin-Pot Foreign General and the Old Iron Woman (1983)

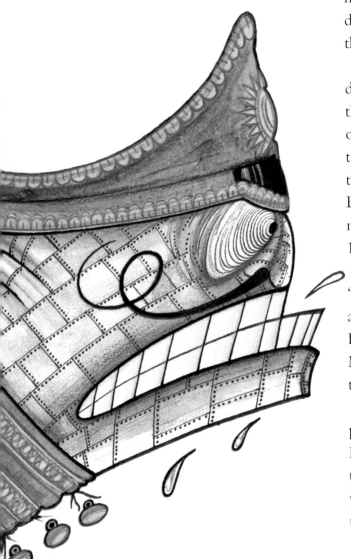

After the publication of *The Tin-Pot Foreign General and the Old Iron Woman*, Raymond Briggs was advised by his publisher to go ex-directory, to avoid abusive phone calls. It was a brave book, coming out only a year after the Falklands 'Crisis', when feelings still ran high. (It was not called a 'war' while it was happening, and war was never formally declared.) Briggs side-stepped the xenophobia of tabloid headlines and made a powerful political statement about the human cost of war, and the arrogant self-interest of national leaders. His book had the force to move all but the most hardened nationalists and, despite its topicality, it endures as a historical testament, a memorial to the dead and as a condemnation of greedy territorial disputes.

On 2 April 1982 Argentina, ruled by General Galtieri, invaded disputed islands known to their inhabitants and to the British as the Falklands and to Argentina as Las Malvinas. They lie 300 miles off the Argentine coast, and the invasion prompted a British task force to sail southwards 8,000 miles to oust the Argentine force and reassert the British sovereignty the islanders wanted. Between April and the British victory on 14 June 1982, some 1,000 people were killed. Many more were wounded. The population of the islands at the time was 1,800 people.

Briggs describes the story of the conflict as 'ready-made satire'. 'It was like a fairy tale. There were two giants, larger-than-life and both apparently puffed up with their own pride and vanity. One, Galtieri, the President of Argentina, had been called a 'tin-pot general' and the other, Margaret Thatcher, was nicknamed 'the iron lady', which suggested they were both made of metal. It was Punch and Judy really.'

It was ludicrous but it was also dismaying. 'It was so awful in every possible way,' says Briggs. 'I just couldn't believe it was happening. It exposed the flaw in the nuclear deterrent argument. Possessing these weapons was supposed to mean that no one would dare attack you. In fact, they do attack you because they know you will never dare to use them.'

Just after the conflict, in July 1982, Briggs contributed to a publication called *Authors Take Sides on the Falklands*, involving 100 mainly British authors. Briggs argued as follows: 'If the Falklands are so important to the British, it would be interesting to know why the Falkland Islanders lost their British nationality under the 1981 Nationality Bill; why they have no MP; why they are not entitled to a British pension; why they get all their major education in Argentina; and also, if the regime is so bad, how is it that several thousand British people have chosen to live there? If the regime is so corrupt why have the British, for years, been selling them arms and training their servicemen?

'This issue was not worth the sacrifice of one single life. Now there is the irony that the Argentines did not harm a single Falklander, but three have died, all killed by the British.'

These three deaths are mentioned in Briggs's book. 'Nobody,' it says, with heavy irony, 'was to blame.' The three were killed accidentally by British fire. Driven by indignation at the pointless waste of these and so many other lives, Briggs was moved to write and draw.

After publication, Briggs did get a few hostile anonymous letters; one, for instance, called it a 'squalid little book'. He was surprised he received so few. Meanwhile the book was used at a rehabilitation centre for Falklands soldiers recovering from battle trauma. They were encouraged to do artwork that expressed their feelings, and used Briggs's book as a starting point.

'I didn't want to ridicule the efforts of the soldiers,' says Briggs. 'I was worried about offending them and their families.' In fact the book is entirely on the side of the soldiers themselves: it is the warmongers in power that come out of it the villains.

The book is remarkable for its use of contrasting styles of artwork, a device which has astonishing emotional impact. The general and the iron woman (Galtieri and Thatcher) are portrayed as extreme caricatures with a satirical savagery reminiscent of the style of the political cartoonist Ralph Steadman. They are made of plates of metal, have crazy eyes drawn in concentric circles and they slaver and smoke. Galtieri has spurs and military insignia. Mrs Thatcher (complete with pearl earrings) has shoes like the Wicked Witch of the West in *The Wizard of Oz*, and a similarly destructive fury. Both are drawn with ink and brash watercolour, and no holds barred. Briggs jokes about the Old Iron Woman's 'war chests' as gold pours out of her hinged breasts.

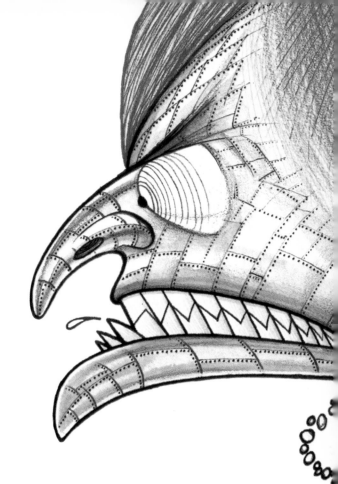

(The war cost £1.6 billion; almost a million pounds for every inhabitant of the Falklands, not counting the cost of subsequent security.)

The book was published, like the later *Wally* books, in an interlude when Julia MacRae, for reasons that had to do with the moves of her own career, was not Briggs's editor. She rightly recognizes that she has been something of a restraining influence on Briggs. His harshest work has been produced without her moderation. She thinks she might have asked him to tone down the satirical cartoons in this book – especially the sexualized imagery of Mrs Thatcher, with her breasts shooting fire and her iron suspender belt. Nevertheless, she feels that their 'over-the-top' vehemence was entirely justified by the contrast they strike with the quiet pencil drawings that follow, expressing the tragic fate of the common soldiers.

After the fury of the protagonists builds to an explosive climax, the next page has a breathtaking shift in tone. The colour has been drained from the pictures. The fairy tale evaporates. The satire becomes real life. The actual consequences of the outrageous competitive bombast are felt. The drawings are muted grey pencil, and there are no more jokes in the text. 'Some men were shot . . . Some men were burned alive . . . Some men were blown to bits . . .'

The second climax of the book is the spread of rows of crosses, captioned: 'Hundreds of brave men were killed. And they were all real men, made of flesh and blood. They were not made of Tin or of Iron.' This moment of mourning encapsulates the message of the book, although it goes on to show the aftermath, interweaving the two styles it has established. The mad looking metal-plated victor sings (quoting Mrs Thatcher), 'Rejoice!' and her belly is swollen as if for her the war was a kind of fruitful consummation. Certainly the patriotic fervour aroused by the Falklands helped Mrs Thatcher to a crushing electoral victory the following year. After the conflict, the 'sad little island', scarred by war, is no better off. We return to the grey pencil for the return of the bodies and the grief of the wounded and bereaved. Sometimes both styles appear on one page: a posthumous medal has a garish ribbon and a bleak, pencil-grey medallion, as if it carries an image of desolation. The Old Iron Woman appears insane and burning red on television as the family of a maimed soldier watch, drawn in muted grey.

Once upon a time, down at the bottom of the world,
there was a sad little island.

No one lived on the sad little island except for a
few poor shepherds.
These poor shepherds spent all their time

counting their sheep and eating them.
They had mutton for breakfast, mutton for dinner
and mutton for tea.

Next door to the sad little island was a great big
kingdom, ruled over by a Wicked Foreign General.

This Wicked Foreign General had wicked foreign
moustachios, and although he had lots of gold on
his hat, he was not real. He was made of Tin Pots.

Now, this Tin-Pot Foreign General wanted to be
Important. He wanted to do something Historical,
so that his name would be printed in all the
big History Books.

So, one day, he got all his soldiers and all his guns
and he put them into boats. Then he sailed them
over the sea to the sad little island.

There he stamped ashore and bagsied
the sad little island for his very own.

"Mea baggazza el islandio!"
(I bags the island!) he roared.

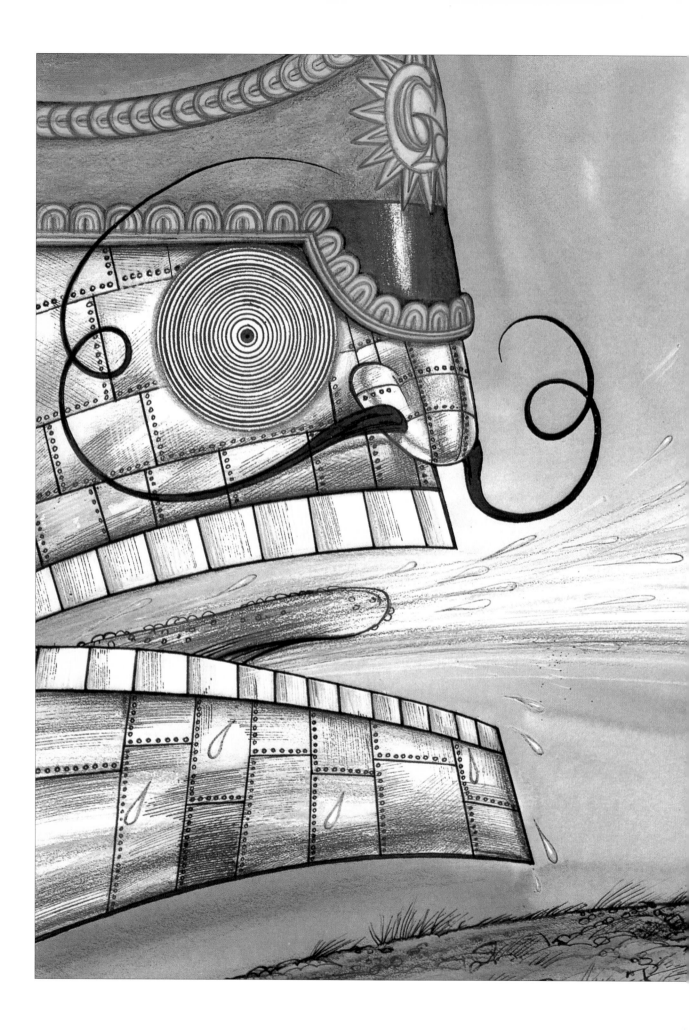

The poor shepherds did not like this at all, because the Tin-Pot Foreign General started bossing them about.

Now listen! Far away over the sea there lived
an old woman with lots of money and guns.

Like the Tin-Pot Foreign General,
she was not real, either. She was made of Iron.

When this Old Iron Woman heard that the Tin-Pot
Foreign General had bagsied the sad little island,
she flew into a rage.

"It's MINE!" she screeched. "MINE! MINE! MINE!
I bagsied it AGES ago! I bagsied it FIRST!
DID! DID! DID!"

She poured out tons of treasure from her huge chest and bought lots and lots of boats.

Then she got all her soldiers and guns and she put them into the boats and sailed them over the sea to the sad little island.

She wanted to bagsy the sad little island back again,
you see.

BANG! BANG! BANG!
went the guns of the Tin-Pot Foreign General.

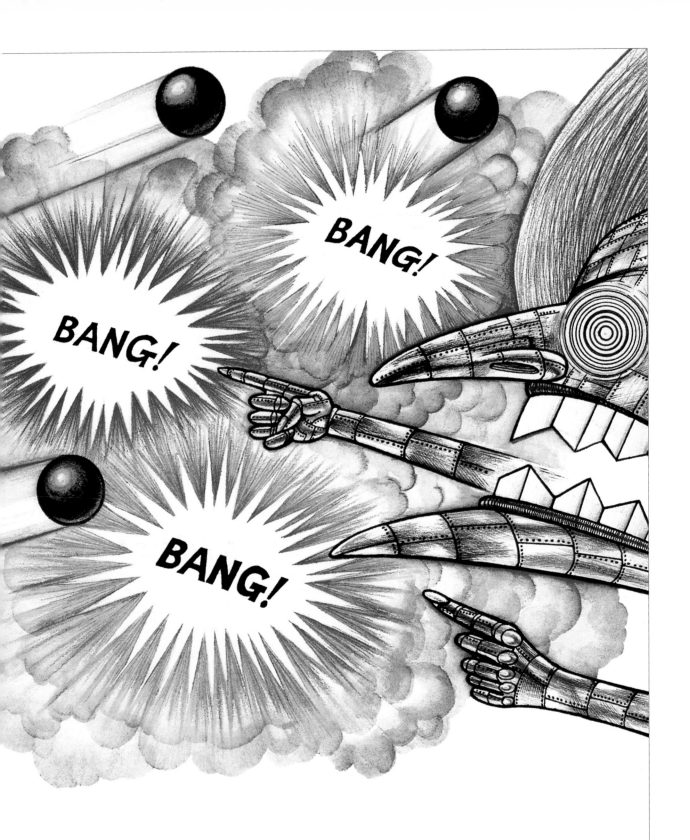

BANG! BANG! BANG!
went the guns of the Old Iron Woman.

Some men were shot.

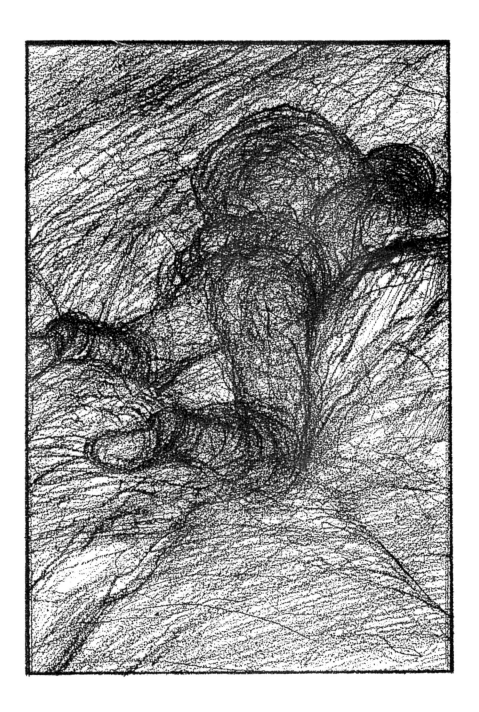

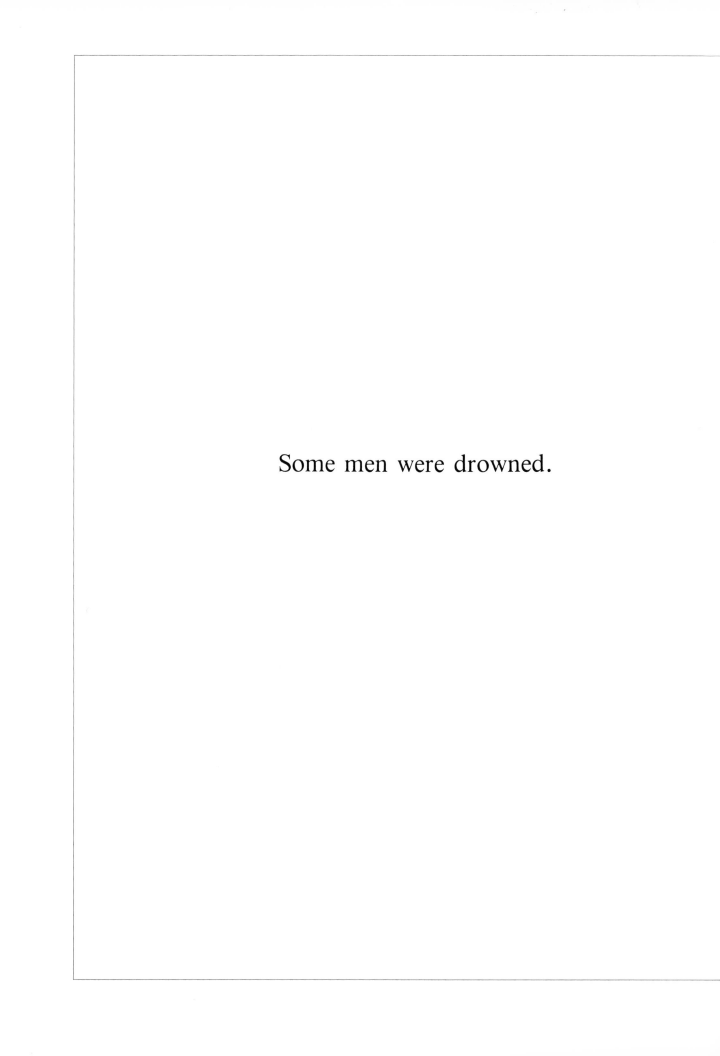

Some men were drowned.

Some men were burned alive.

Some men were blown to bits.

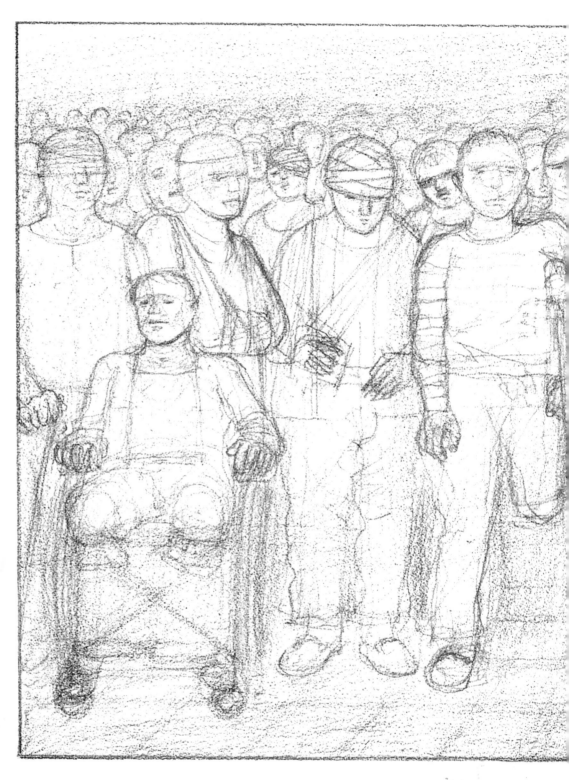

Some men were only half blown to bits and

ame home with parts of their bodies missing.

Hundreds of brave men were killed. And they

re all real men, made of flesh and blood.
      They were not made of Tin or of Iron.

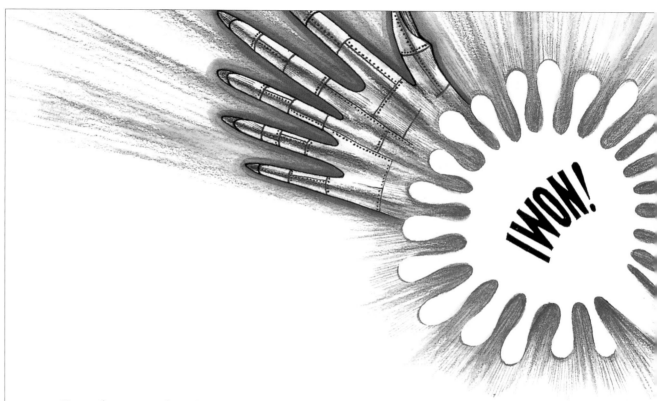

In the end, the Old Iron Woman's soldiers
beat the Tin-Pot Foreign General's soldiers and
the Tin-Pot Foreign General's soldiers ran away.

"I WON!" sang the Old Iron Woman. "REJOICE!"

"Mei villi ritorno!" (I will return!) swore the
Tin-Pot Foreign General.

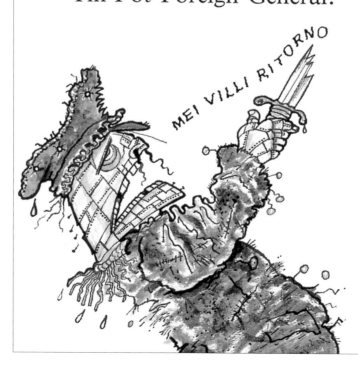

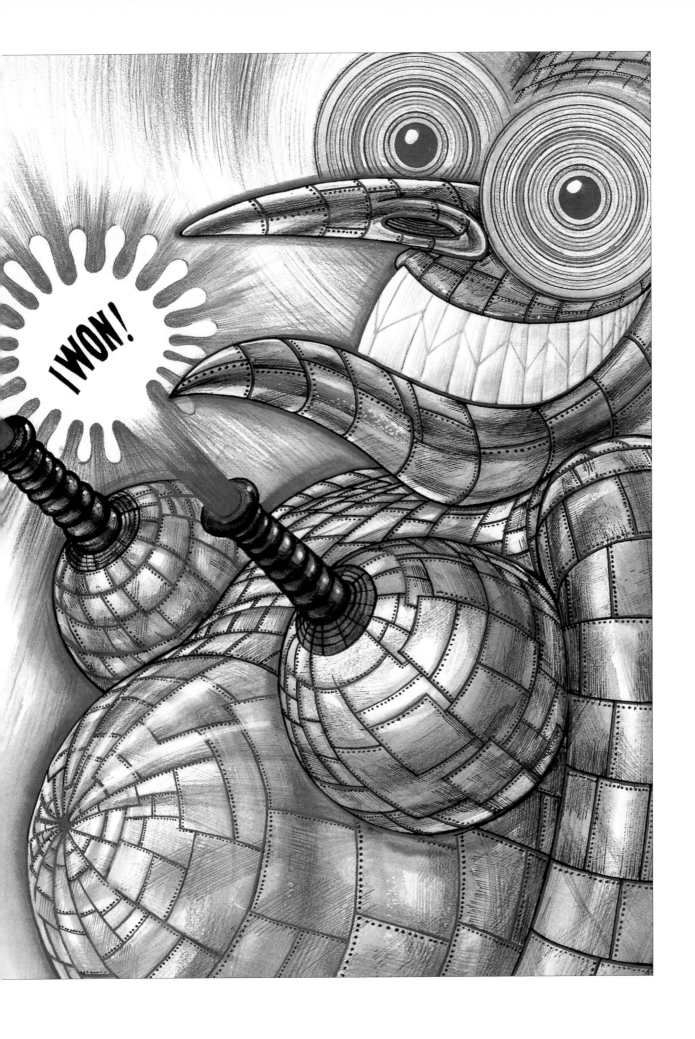

So the poor shepherds on the sad little island went
on counting their sheep and eating them.
They had mutton for breakfast, mutton for dinner

and mutton for tea.
Three of them were killed in the battle, but no one
was to blame.

Later on, a boat came back to the Old Iron Woman

ingdom with a big iron box full of dead bodies.

Then the Old Iron Woman gave all her soldier:

a special medal.

After this, there was a Grand Parade to celebrate the Grea

Victory and everyone went to Church and Thanked God.

But the soldiers with bits of their bodies missing were not invited to take part in the Grand Parade, in case the sight of them spoiled the rejoicing. Some watched from a grandstand and others stayed at home with their memories and their medals.

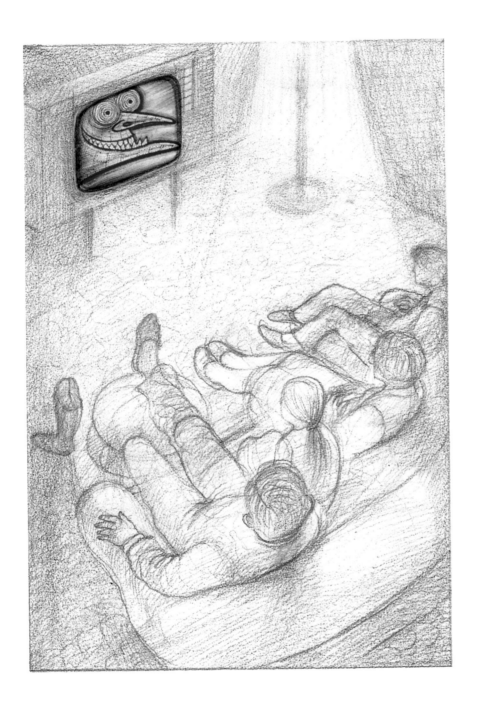

And the families of the dead tended the graves.

Briggs was shocked at the fact that the wounded soldiers were not brought into the victory celebrations or invited to the service of thanksgiving – 'In case,' as the book puts it, 'the sight of them spoiled the rejoicing' – and integrated this dismaying fact into the book.

His final frame: 'And the families of the dead tended the graves,' contains the classic Briggsian device of figures, including a small boy, drawn from the back – so much more expressive of grief than full-face agony. Briggs has brought home the message of his opening epigraphs, from Einstein, that 'Nationalism is an infantile disease. It is the measles of mankind', and from Dr Johnson that 'Patriotism is the last refuge of a scoundrel'. And he has made his point that the conflict was 'not worth the sacrifice of a single life'. The book was in the *Sunday Times* bestseller list for eleven weeks, the first four weeks at number one.

Ethel and Ernest: A True Story
(1998)

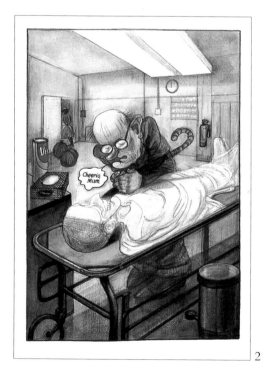

1. *Ethel and Ernest*
2. *Unlucky Wally: Twenty Years On*

'Raymond's parents are with him every day of his life,' says Julia MacRae. They, and the world they lived in, recur in his work, and when his record of his parents' life together, *Ethel and Ernest*, was published it felt like a key to all that had gone before. One critic identified it as 'the book Briggs was always trying to write'.

Ernest, the Co-op milkman who was the inspiration for Briggs's *Father Christmas*, and who had a walk-on part in the book, was now fleshed out. Ethel was already familiar from the drawings of Wally's mother, and the boy's in *The Snowman*, and of Hilda in *Gentleman Jim* and *When the Wind Blows*, who had something of Ethel's fastidiousness and her innocence. Both parents' faces can be identified on characters in Briggs's early illustrations: the crooked man in *The Mother Goose Treasury*, for instance, looks like Ernest. Even Fungus's face had Ethel's features. Now the memoir told the story of one of the houses depicted in *Father Christmas*; it was in Ashen Grove, Wimbledon Park, and Briggs's parents had occupied it for forty-one years. The wartime memories of Jim and Hilda in *When the Wind Blows* – of the Anderson shelter painted green and decorated with nasturtiums, and the Morrison shelter – turned out to come from Briggs's own childhood. The distressing circumstances of Ethel's corpse in hospital confirmed the autobiographical element in the *Unlucky Wally* books; we had seen the same sad episode involving Wally's mother in *Unlucky Wally: Twenty Years On*. Themes of class and generations divided by a difference in education – which were explored in *Gentleman Jim* and *The Man*, and even hinted at in *Jim and the Beanstalk* – were revealed to derive from Briggs's own experience of being educated beyond his parents' comprehension: 'I hope he won't get too posh for us,' worries Ernest when his son gets into grammar school. (This theme of parents and children divided by intellect was to appear again in *Ug*.) So many elements of Briggs's work can be traced back to sources in the story of his parents.

Many regard *Ethel and Ernest* as Briggs's masterpiece. It elevated the strip illustration to the stature of literature. One critic (Blake Morrison) thought if it hadn't been non-fiction it would have been a contender for the Booker Prize. It is a tender and moving personal tribute, and also a social history of the 1920s–1970s, chronicling changing attitudes and habits, domestic details, technological developments and political events. It is, as the critic Philip Hensher put it, 'Briggs using his art not just to entertain but to instruct.' Ethel and Ernest's particular experience illuminates the times they live through.

One of the book's dominant themes is class, and social aspiration. Ethel is thrilled to have a bathroom, a son who goes to grammar school and, eventually, her own (humble) office job, as these are markers of social standing. Although she is a former lady's maid, from a family of thirteen who lived in a small terrace house, and is married to a milkman whose family were rougher than hers, she is outraged at the suggestion that she might be working class. In one poignant exchange, Ernest reads aloud from the paper that the average family needs £6 a week to stay above the poverty line. 'What's the poverty line?' asks Ethel. 'Dunno,' says Ernest, 'I just wish I earned £6 a week.' Ethel nevertheless speaks of the working class as 'they'.

Ethel picked up airs, says Briggs, from her job as a maid. 'Working for posh people, she discovered fish knives and side plates. Dad [as we see in the book] was always being told off for waving his spoon in the air.' She has a horror of the common, which includes wearing boots instead of shoes and having visible pipes in the house.

Ernest, who recognizes his own class and does not share his wife's enthusiasm for a white collar job, thinks of himself as a working man, and a part of the working man's fight for social justice. He votes Labour. Ethel thinks this is socially demeaning, and shushes her son when he confesses to a similar allegiance. Her support for Churchill and conservatism are, as she sees it, an expression of her refinement. Ernest regards the post-war election victory for Labour, the Welfare State and nationalization as milestones in the Struggle that he is part of. He has some sympathy with his Communist brother.

Social and political attitudes are interwoven with national and international events: growing unemployment, the rise of Hitler, IRA bombs in England in 1939, the outbreak of war, evacuation of the children (heartbreaking for Ethel), the bombing of the Docklands (the horrors that Ernest witnesses are incompletely articulated, but his tears say everything), VE Day, Hiroshima, the Korean War, post-war rationing; the Cold War, the moon landing, decimalization. Each of these events is made vivid by Ethel and Ernest's personal and particular reactions. Sometimes these are humorous, such as Ethel's naïveté about Hitler. When she hears that the proceeds from the British publication of *Mein Kampf* are going to the Red Cross she remarks, 'That's nice of him.' When Ernest tells her: 'Here Et, did you know if you're a Jew in Germany you're forbidden to marry a German,' Ethel, missing the point sublimely, says, 'I'd hate to marry a German.' Ill and old, she is unimpressed by the moon landing. Astronauts taking pebbles home are, she thinks, 'just like kiddies at the seaside'. And a comical exchange about decimalization empathizes with the confusion this purportedly simple change in the currency engendered in a generation of elderly people.

Sometimes, though, Ethel is astute. Proving that she is not exactly like Hilda in *When the Wind Blows*, she demonstrates a grasp of the implications of nuclear conflict. The atom bomb will, she says, put an end to wars . . . 'You can't fight a war with bombs like that. Everyone will be dead the first day.'

Ethel's reactions to new technology are, through our eyes, comical and ironic. At the astonishing news that television is to be broadcast for a whole one and a half hours a night, she says, as she busies herself with housework, 'I suppose it might be all right for the gentry.' At the same time she reminds us that there was a time when things we now take for granted were remarkable; when, for instance, a person could wonder what a fridge was for, and when a gas copper was a luxury, since it provided hot water at the strike of a match, even though doing the laundry in it still involved pounding, rinsing, scrubbing with a brush, wringing and mangling. She is in awe too of the phone. 'When my parents first got their telephone,' says Briggs, 'they were quite nervous of it. They would almost stand to attention if it rang.'

Sometimes the personal and particular make historical events the more poignant. A doodlebug too close for comfort leaves Ernest and Raymond face down in the cabbages of their allotment. A bomb causes damage to the Briggses' house two days after Raymond has been sent away to safety. On VE Day, Ernest tries to jolly along a glum participant, who reminds him that he lost his son in the war. Ernest discovers that a boy who used to help him on his milk round grew up to be killed in Korea.

Along with the incidents that mark the way the world was changing, the book tells personal anecdotes of the kind that all families tell about themselves. These self-sufficient little episodes

include Ethel's dismay when Raymond had his first haircut; the day little Raymond came all the way home from school to go to the lavatory; the day, to his mother's mortification, he was brought home by the police; as well as a story Ethel never knew, the time a man on Ernest's milk round tried to persuade him to have sex with his wife. 'He turned the proposition down, of course,' says Briggs.

It was one such anecdote that triggered the whole book. Briggs 'loved the way they met by chance'. Ernest, happening to cycle past, waved back cheekily when he saw a pretty girl shaking a duster out of a window. This brought Ernest into Ethel's life, and it gave their son a way into their biography.

Ethel & Ernest

Sometimes, as in this opening sequence, the pictures alone tell the story. And we do not hear in the text, for example, about such wartime concepts as 'Make Do and Mend', but we see Ethel mending a sock and Ernest resoling a shoe as they talk. Their place and time is in the details of the pictures but so too is much of their character and their relationship: Ernest lies sprawled upside down on the three-piece suite he has just brought home; he is physically more casual and boyish than his wife. In confirmation of this, Briggs remembers how his father 'used to tap-dance on a patch of lino in the kitchen in his hobnailed boots . . . It was terribly loud and heavy.' He also 'used to run downstairs at breakneck speed'. His son inherited the habit.

Meanwhile Briggs's own feeling about his first school uniform is all in his little boy's face. And his father's death, and the pains that built up to it, are told in four wordless frames.

Inevitably, this is partly Briggs's own story, but he was reluctant to include himself. 'I had to be in the story, too. I didn't want to be in it. I put myself in it as little as possible. But I was their only child, after all.' There was no escaping either the inclusion of his late wife Jean. 'Well, she was their daughter-in-law, she had to be there.' In fact he and Jean serve the useful function of representing his generation, which was puzzling to his parents. Raymond, the art school student with the long hair his mother was always longing to comb, and the van she disapproved of (it suggested blue collar work), embodies in the book the changing fashions and mores of the 1960s. The book has to hand over to them in the end. On the last page Raymond and Jean stand in his parents' garden, in front of the pear tree Raymond grew from a pip. It suggests the cycle of life, but this was unintentional. 'I meant no symbolism. It just happened. We stood in front of the pear tree, like that.'

Julia MacRae made a few changes when she saw the dummy of this book, although the three years Briggs had spent on it meant that it was perfect in most of its details. She divided the pages, which had been one continuous narrative, into decades, to simplify things for the reader. Now we know which point in history the story has reached. She also toned down two pages. The image of Raymond's agonizing arrival is, though still accompanied by a tremendous cry, slightly more blurred around the business end of the birth than in the original. And one picture, on the page with Ethel and Ernest's wedding photograph, was replaced at her suggestion. Below the wedding photo, Briggs's dummy had a drawing of the consummation, which suggested that it was a painful and unhappy experience. It would have made the point that this was a time when couples did not have sex until their wedding night. But it was, says MacRae, too harsh an image for this stage in the book. 'We did not yet know them well enough.' It was replaced with a romantic photograph from their honeymoon in Hastings, of the two of them sitting together on the 'Lovers' Seat'. Only Ethel's uncertain smile hints at what was in the picture this replaced.

'I tried to portray their lives in a way that wouldn't offend them if they had been alive,' says Briggs. 'Except for the end, of course, when they both die. That was very difficult for me to draw. I would only spend about ten or fifteen minutes a day doing it – I couldn't manage more than that. It was very hard to portray my mother on a trolley in a hospital annexe, but that's an important part of it all. We're so nervous of death nowadays and prefer not to acknowledge it. I feel that's an issue for children too – they need to realize that life doesn't go on and on. Living "happily ever after" in fairy stories doesn't actually mean that.'

Philip Hensher said of Briggs's work in general that 'his world lies

Three pages from this book illustrate one unchanging element in the life of Ethel and Ernest – the Wimbledon Park house in which they lived – shown first at the time of purchase, then during the devastation of war, and finally in the seventies, when Raymond says farewell to his boyhood home after the death of his parents

between glorious anarchy and the frank virtue of the respectable English working classes.' This book *is* a celebration of the English working classes, asserting that ordinary lives warrant detailed attention. It strives to tell the truth and refuses to aggrandize or sentimentalize.

'It's just a book of facts, just their plain lives,' says Briggs. 'Nothing extraordinary about them, nothing dramatic; no divorce or anything. But they were my parents and I wanted to remember them.'

Briggs said that he thought nobody would buy *Ethel and Ernest* but in fact the book sold 33,000 copies in the first few weeks after publication and went on to sell over 100,000. Among the languages the book was translated into were Welsh and Japanese. 'I honestly didn't think this book would appeal to anybody when I wrote it. It was a biography of two people that the public hadn't heard of. I'm amazed it struck a chord with so many people.' Many of them wrote to say so. 'I have lost count of the number of letters I received from people who grew up in the war years and remember similar events with their parents.' He exclaims at 'a book about my mum and dad up there in the bestseller lists amongst all the football biographies and dictionaries! They'd be proud of me for that, of course, but probably rather embarrassed too. I imagine they would say, "It wasn't like that," or "How can you talk about that?"'

Ethel and Ernest was the Illustrated Book of the Year at the British Book Awards. Schools now use it as a set text, to illuminate twentieth-century history. When Briggs saw a photograph of his parents on a television programme about the book, he cried. 'I hadn't cried since they had died. It was something to do with their size on the screen – so big. It was as if they were still alive.'

Ethel and Ernest on their wedding day

BIBLIOGRAPHY

1958

Peter and the Piskies: Cornish Folk and Fairy Tales Ruth Manning-Sanders (OUP); *The Wonderful Cornet* Barbara Ker Wilson (Hamish Hamilton)

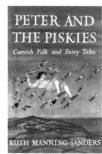

1959

The Missing Scientist Sydney Frank Stevens (OUP); *The Onion Man* Alan Ross (Hamish Hamilton); *Peter's Busy Day* A. Stephen Tring (Hamish Hamilton)

1960

Danger on Glass Island Alan Ross (Hamish Hamilton); *Look at Castles* Alfred Duggan (Hamish Hamilton)

1961

Look at Churches Alfred Duggan (Hamish Hamilton); *Midnight Adventure* (Hamish Hamilton); *The Strange House* (Hamish Hamilton)

1962

The Fair to Middling Arthur Calder-Marshall (Penguin); *Ring-a-Ring o' Roses* (Hamish Hamilton)

1963

Sledges to the Rescue (Hamish Hamilton); *The Study Book of Houses* Clifford Warburton (Bodley Head); *The White Land* (Hamish Hamilton); *William's Wild Day Out* Meriol Trevor (Hamish Hamilton)

1964

Fee Fi Fo Fum: a Picture Book of Nursery Rhymes (Hamish Hamilton); *The Swan Princess* unattributed text (Nelson); *Whistling Rufus* William Mayne (Hamish Hamilton);

The Hamish Hamilton Book of Myths and Legends Jacynth Hope-Simpson (ed.) (Hamish Hamilton)

1965

The Hamish Hamilton Book of Magical Beasts Ruth Manning-Sanders (ed.) (Hamish Hamilton); *Stevie* Elfrida Vipont (Hamish Hamilton); *The Wreck of Moni* Alan Ross (Hamish Hamilton)

1966

The Flying 19 James Aldridge (Hamish Hamilton); *The Mother Goose Treasury* (Hamish Hamilton); *The Way Over Windle* Mabel Esther Allan (Methuen)

1968

The Christmas Book James Reeves (ed.) (Heinemann); *The Hamish Hamilton Book of Giants* William Mayne (ed.) (Hamish Hamilton); *Jimmy Murphy and the White Duesenberg* Bruce Carter (Hamish Hamilton); *Lindbergh the Lone Flyer* Nicholas Fisk (Hamish Hamilton); *Nuvolari and the Alfa Romeo* Bruce Carter (Hamish Hamilton); *Poems for Me, Books 4 & 5* Kit Patrickson (Ginn); *Richthofen the Red Baron* Nicholas Fisk (Hamish Hamilton)

1969

The Elephant and the Bad Baby Elfrida Vipont (Hamish Hamilton); *First Up Everest* Showell Styles (Hamish Hamilton); *Shackleton's Epic Voyage* Michael Brown (Hamish Hamilton); *This Little Puffin: Finger Plays and Nursery Games* Elizabeth Matterson (ed.), chapter head illustrations by Raymond Briggs, decorations by David Woodroffe (Penguin)

1970

Jim and the Beanstalk (Hamish Hamilton); *The Tale of Three Landlubbers* Ian Serraillier (Hamish Hamilton)

1972

The Fairy Tale Treasury Virginia Haviland (ed.) (Hamish Hamilton); *Festivals* Ruth Manning-Sanders (ed.) (Heinemann)

1973

Father Christmas (Hamish Hamilton); *The Forbidden Forest, and Other Stories* James Reeves (Heinemann)

1975

Father Christmas goes on Holiday (Hamish Hamilton)

1977

Fungus the Bogeyman (Hamish Hamilton)

1978

The Snowman (Hamish Hamilton)

1980

Gentleman Jim (Hamish Hamilton)

1982

The Fungus the Bogeyman Plop-Up Book (Hamish Hamilton); *When the Wind Blows* (Hamish Hamilton)

1983

When the Wind Blows (play, adapted by Raymond Briggs, unillustrated) (French)

Above: cartoon by Trog (Wally Fawkes), *Observer*, 8 February 1987

1984

The Tin-Pot Foreign General and the Old Iron Woman (Hamish Hamilton)

1985

The Snowman Pop-Up Book (a pop-up book with music) with Ron van der Meer (Hamish Hamilton)

1987

Unlucky Wally (Hamish Hamilton)

1988

Unlucky Wally: Twenty Years On (Hamish Hamilton)

1992

The Man (Julia MacRae Books)

1994

The Bear (Julia MacRae Books)

1998

Ethel and Ernest (Cape)

2001

Ug: Boy Genius of the Stone Age (Cape); *The Adventures of Bert* Allan Ahlberg (Puffin)

2002

A Bit More Bert Allan Ahlberg (Puffin)

2004

The Puddleman (Cape)

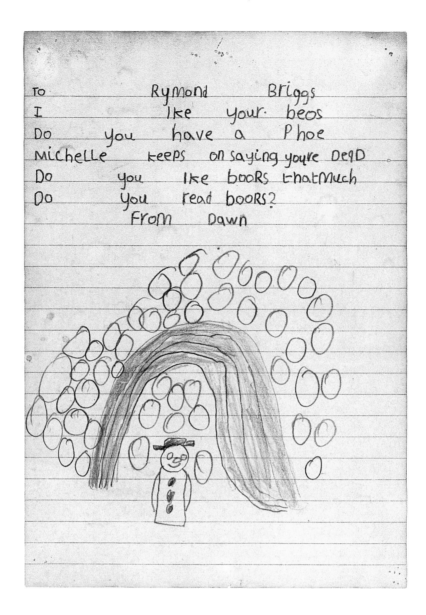

TO Rymond Briggs
I lke your beos
Do you have a Phoe
Michelle keeps on saying you're DeaD
Do you lke booRs thatMuch
Do you read booRS?
From Dawn

ACKNOWLEDGEMENTS

The author and publishers would like to thank the following for their kind permission to reproduce material:

Allan Ahlberg and Fritz Wegner for *The Better Brown Stories* p.105; Steve Bell for *The Snoreman* p.114; The Bodley Head for cover and illustration from *The Study Book of Houses* by Clifford Warburton p.19; The Bridgeman Art Library for detail from Brueghel's *Children's Games*, Kunsthistorisches Museum, Vienna p.166; *Snowman* merchandise by kind permission of the Copyrights Group p.115; Egmont Books Ltd for illustrations from *The Way Over Windle* by Mabel Esther Allan, published by Methuen © 1966 pp. 17,18; Wally Fawkes (Trog) for cartoon p.287; Zul Mukhida, photographer, pp. (ix)-(xi); Julia MacRae for Birthday Card and Fungus inscription pp. 156 & 179; The Estate of Ruth Manning-Sanders, author, for illustrations from *Peter and the Piskies* p.16; *Private Eye* for the *The Snoreman* p.114 and *Lookalike* p.180 © Pressdram Limited 2002/1993; Ryan Vincent for illustration, *Raymond Briggs Charecters* p.163.

Raymond Briggs titles originally published by Hamish Hamilton: *Midnight Adventure, The Strange House, Ring-a-Ring o' Roses, Sledges to the Rescue, The White Land, Fee Fi Fo Fum, The Mother Goose Treasury, Jim and the Beanstalk, The Fairy Tale Treasury, Father Christmas, Father Christmas goes on Holiday, Fungus the Bogeyman, The Snowman, Gentleman Jim, The Fungus the Bogeyman Plop-up Book, When the Wind Blows, The Tin-Pot Foreign General and the Old Iron Woman, The Snowman Pop-Up Book, Unlucky Wally, Unlucky Wally: Twenty Years On*
Published by Puffin: *The Adventures of Bert, A Bit More Bert*
Published by Julia MacRae Books: *The Man, The Bear*
Published by Jonathan Cape: *Ethel and Ernest, Ug: Boy Genius of the Stone Age, The Puddleman*

Every effort has been made to trace the holders of copyright material in this book. If any query should arise it should be addressed to the publishers.